SCENT OF SUSPICION

SCENT OF SUSPICION

A Novel

IRENE HUGHES

Library of Congress Control Number:		2006901692
ISBN :	Hardcover	1-4257-1062-X
	Softcover	1-4257-1061-1

This book was printed in the United States of America.

Front Cover by Jim Hall

To order additional copies of this book, contact:
Xlibris Corporation
1-888-795-4274
www.Xlibris.com
Orders@Xlibris.com
33542

For Ruth Dollens Chiles,
whose friendship has lasted
since college days—
in spite of me—
and whose talent and humour
enrich my life.

~

And for Mary Owen Roberts,
whose faith and support
mean more than she knows.

The real estate "sleuths" of the author's previous novel, *Sign In For Murder,* once again land in a crime investigation! The kidnapping of Town Mountain Realty's secretary-agent quickly becomes linked to the murder of a friend of broker Blair Camfield. Chief Investigator Ned Washburn includes Blair in some of his detective work—and immediately romantic fire ignites between them.

Broker Landis Galleher is off on a cruise with Peter Mason, whom she met at the end of the previous year's murder case, but returns in time to involve herself in the kidnapping-murder investigation and to meddle in the budding romance of her realty partner.

During the preliminary hearing for an arrested suspect, the "sleuths" discover the main clues that nail the case.

ACKNOWLEDGMENTS

The writing of *Scent of Suspicion* was quite a bit more "stretched" out than anticipated, and there were a few times when I was tempted to abandon the effort altogether. However, friends and many readers of my previous novel (*Sign In For Murder*) nudged me along and are credited with the completion of this novel.

Especially to Ruby Dodd, Martha Tinnell, Pat Price, Elaine Hooker, and Ella Browning go my thanks and deep appreciation for their continuing encouragement and loyal support—as well as for editorial comments and suggestions.

For valuable technical contributions my thanks go to Jim Hall, Shelvia Allen Hall, Tyler Price, Leon Brandt, Basil J. Clark, Caitlin Price, Rosemary North, Polly Harvey, and Debbie Tyree.

ONE

The phone rang just as Blair poured her second glass of wine. She glanced at her watch. And frowned. It was 6:30. She detested phone calls when she was preparing dinner. "If this is a telemarketer," she mumbled, "he's gonna be told where to stuff it!"

"HAL-LO," she answered brusquely.

"Blair, sorry to bother you. Do you know where Mom is?" It was Page, the daughter of her secretary-agent, now a day student at Sweet Briar College. Her voice sounded flat, much more serious than was characteristic.

"No. Not now. Why? Is something wrong?"

"No. Well . . . I don't know. She always phones when she's going to be late. And she hasn't. I called the office, got voice mail. Called her cell phone, got a recording that it was not in service. I was just wondering . . ." Page trailed off.

"Page, all I can tell you is that she had an appointment to show a property east of Howardsville this afternoon. In Albemarle County. Customer was to meet her there at 3:00. She left the office a little after 2:00. I haven't talked to her since. Do you think maybe she stopped to have a drink—or to visit someone?"

"Maybe. But, still, I think she would have called."

"Have you been home all the time since . . . say, 4:00?"

"Yes. But even if I hadn't been, we have Caller ID."

"Huumm . . ." Blair mused, unconsciously drumming her fingers on the counter-top and taking a sip of wine. "Tell you what, Page. I'll drive down to that property. She might be there still—maybe can't get cell reception. And you know how Lauren likes to talk. Could be the customer is a single guy!" Blair quipped.

Page chuckled hesitantly, sounding unconvinced that Blair's scenario was plausible but acknowledging that it was generally apropos for her mother, a forty-year-old divorcee. "You'll go?" she asked, slight relief obvious in her voice. "That *would* help."

"Sure. I'll phone you from there. Okay? Meanwhile, you call any of her friends whom you know. And try not to worry, Page. I'm sure she has an explanation."

Blair hung up, started to swill the wine left in her glass, then quickly plunked it down. Wouldn't do to drink and drive.

"Richard, Lauren's daughter can't locate her mom. I'm going to the Bannister property—you know, the one a little beyond Howardsville. Lauren went to show it this afternoon. Will you take over dinner prep? I should be back by 8:15 or so," Blair said, addressing her husband, who was sitting in his recliner in the den watching the TV evening news and having a before-dinner drink. "If there's a delay, I'll phone."

"Sure. But don't go alone. Those backroads are pretty deserted. Take Whitley." Whitley was their eleven-year-old son.

"Okay. We'll take Doby, too," she said, referring to their Doberman, one of five family dogs, as she left the room to find Whitley.

Wednesday, October 9, 6:45, Eastern-daylight time. Blair knew she wouldn't have time to make the fifty mile round-trip before dark. It would be comforting to have Whitley along. Niggling thoughts were beginning to press in. Not strong enough to be foreboding exactly, but definitely disquieting.

To be unaccountable was not characteristic of Lauren. Quite the contrary. Lauren was always prompt, always considerate of others' time, and she always left messages pertaining to her schedule and whereabouts. True, she could have had car trouble. But it would be a rather long-shot coincidence to have cell-phone trouble at the same time. Of course, she might be where there was poor reception. Or none. Or maybe, joking aside, she *had* gone somewhere for a drink with the customer. The property wasn't too far from Scottsville—or, for that matter, no more than twenty miles from Charlottesville.

So went Blair's thoughts as she drove the narrow, winding road through heavily forested areas. Blair and her partner, Landis Galleher, had hired Lauren the previous year to be receptionist-secretary for their real estate company, Town Mountain Realty. At that time they had been heavily involved with the investigation of a murder which had occurred in one of their listed houses. Their activities in seeking the murderer's identity had kept them away from the office so much that, for a fledgling operation also suddenly swamped with increased sales activity, they had desperately needed some office help. Almost immediately Lauren had enrolled in real estate classes and subsequently passed the state exam for a sales representative license. She still served as receptionist-secretary, while dealing with customers on a part-time basis. Congeniality and keen people-skills served her well in sales activity, and she loved the work. As well, the extra income eased her struggle to provide for her family.

"MOM, don't drive *so* fast!" Whitley screamed, jerking upright from his Game Boy play when Blair hugged a curve so hard that his thin body bumped into the door, despite his tightly buckled seat belt.

"Sorry, son."

Blair wasn't very familiar with the road. In fact, she had travelled it no more than twice in her twelve years living in the area. And one of those times was with Lauren at the wheel when Lauren had taken her to the property to assist with drawing up her first listing contract. The property had been part of a large farm purchased by a timber company. In turn, the timber company had surveyed off ten acres containing the large old farmhouse and several outbuildings and offered the package for re-sale.

They encountered very little traffic during the twenty-five mile trip. After all, it was dinner-time generally, as well as a week day. At 7:25 they pulled into the driveway of the old farmhouse, situated on a knoll three-hundred feet off the secondary road.

"Mom, nobody's here," Whitley said, echoing her quick assessment.

"Looks that way. But let's check out the house anyway, now that we're here."

"Oh, Mom, what's the use? Let's go home," he complained.

"Whitley, come on!" Blair commanded, looking into his eyes directly before closing the car door. "I really need you for back-up. Quick! Bring Doby."

That did the trick. The avid viewer of TV detective programs hit the ground, crouched low to cover her flank. Doby followed, nose to ground. Blair hid her smile and walked swiftly to the wide porch which embraced the full front of the house and wrapped around its side and along the rear wing, making an L. She tried the knobs on three doors. All locked. She peeked through front and side windows. Only empty rooms showed.

Straightening up and exhaling audibly, Whitley exclaimed, "That's a relief!" He stepped off the side porch and started to walk toward the car.

"Whitley, wait," Blair called as she turned to step off the porch. "Let's take a look at the buildings back there," she added, pointing to the area behind the house.

"Oh, Mom! What for?"

"WHITLEY!"

"Oh, all right! But I'm not going in 'em!" Whitley asserted, the real eleven-year-old now surfacing.

Blair walked first to what had probably been a storage shed for garden tools and lawnmowers. The door was partly open. Just a glance revealed that it was empty. Next she looked into a building where some loose feathers and dried manure identified it as a former chicken house. She couldn't help smiling a bit, recalling Lauren's phobia about feathers. "She sure didn't open this door! If she had, I would expect to find her lying here in a dead faint!"

"Why?"

"Because she panics when close to chickens, birds—or just feathers."

"Why?" Children's interminable questions!

"She can't help it, Whitley. It's sort of . . . like a disease."

"Oh . . . ," Whitley mumbled. His expression revealed clearly that he didn't understand, but the word *disease* quelled further questioning.

An inspection of two large buildings, a cow barn and a hay barn by the looks of small fragmented contents in them, turned up nothing obviously disturbed in either. Blair walked slowly along the driveway and parking area, bent forward to more closely examine the dirt and gravel surface. Nothing out of the ordinary showed, no disturbance of dirt or gravel to suggest a struggle or spinning tires.

Back at her car, Blair called Page. "Nothing here, Page. Anything on your end?"

"No. Nobody around here has seen her since lunchtime."

The dull flatness of Page's voice made Blair choke a little. Despite her previous efforts to remain upbeat, anxiety was now taking root. She struggled to keep her own voice calm.

"Page, I'm going to stop by the house that's next door—across a field, less than a quarter mile away. Maybe someone there saw Lauren this afternoon. And I'll also inquire at a convenience store a few miles back. Then I'll phone you again."

Blair switched the phone off and sat gripping the steering wheel and staring straight ahead. Several minutes passed while she was lost in contemplation. Suddenly a loud cracking sound brought her out of her near-trance so violently that one elbow slammed into the horn. That blast jolted her upright, causing her head to crash into the car's roof. The thin headliner offered little cushioning.

"Dammit!" she screeched, rubbing her crown.

Then she saw the culprit. Whitley was standing off to the right, his hand frozen in mid-air by the horn blast. Closer scrutiny revealed a small rock grasped tightly in his fingers. He was poised to throw the rock against the house. A second one.

"Whitley, don't you dare! Get in this car," Blair shouted. When he didn't move, she commanded, "RIGHT NOW!"

The boy shrugged sullenly, pocketed the rock, whistled for the dog, and moved to the car. He opened the rear door for Doby, then as he slid into the front seat, he said, "I wasn't doing nothing."

"Anything," Blair corrected.

"That's right," he agreed. "I wasn't."

Blair did her best to throttle her exasperation—and frustration. "Son, you could have broken a window. As it is, you scared the sh . . . You caused me to hurt my head."

"How did me throwing a little ole gravel do that?" he asked inanely.

"My throwing. I . . . oh, never mind," she conceded wearily. "Landis, who used to love pointing out *my* grammatical boo-boo's, would really get a hoot from listening to my feeble efforts with Whitley!" Blair managed the presence of mind to think.

Sensing an undercurrent of stress in his mother, Whitley quickly grew serious. "I'm sorry, Mom. I just wasn't thinking."

Blair patted his bony knee. "I know, Whitley. It's all right. I'm sorry, too. Just the situation, you know. Let's just get on down the road to the next house."

Whitley remained absolutely quiet during the short drive.

A woman in her fifties opened her door when Blair knocked. She was as tall as Blair, her salt-and-pepper hair cut short. She wore a print apron over a denim dress and was drying her hands with a dish towel.

"Ma'am, I'm Blair Camfield with Town Mountain Realty. We have the property next door listed for sale."

"Yes, I know. Won't you come in?" Such politeness to a perfect stranger certainly said something for the manners—and sense of security—of country women!

"No, thank you. An agent from our office was supposed to show that property this afternoon. I was wondering if you saw her," Blair ventured.

"Saw her? Well, no, not really. I saw cars over there today but I didn't see people," the woman responded.

"How many cars? What time? Do you remember?"

The woman's eyes met Blair's directly, revealing that she had sensed an urgency in Blair's rapid-fire questions.

"Well, now, I'm not exactly sure. Let's see. There was some kind of vehicle over there after dinner—I mean, lunchtime. Maybe around 2:30. Didn't look like a car. Bigger, a dark color . . ."

"How about a little later—around 3:00? Did you see others arrive?"

"Two, I think."

"Both at the same time?" Blair pressed.

"I don't think so. But I can't say definitely."

"Did you hear anything?"

"No. Too far away. Besides, I was indoors."

"Did you see the vehicles leave? All at the same time?"

"Heavens, no! I wasn't paying close attention, Mrs. Camfield, so I don't know when they left. There're vehicles over there nearly every day, actually. Is there a problem of some kind?"

"Mrs.—?"

"Alders."

"Mrs. Alders, I don't know. I hope not. Lauren Michaels, the agent who had an appointment to meet a customer over there at 3:00 today, hasn't returned. Her daughter called me, very concerned."

"Oh, my! That was . . . what . . . five hours ago?"

"I know—"

"What does she look like?"

"Brown hair, brown eyes, about five-four, forty, attractive."

"If I see her, how do I reach you?"

"Here's my card. With home, office, and cell numbers. Thank you, Mrs. Alders. Good-night."

"Good-night. Good luck," Mrs. Alders called to Blair's retreating back.

Blair spun tires as she accelerated out of the Alders driveway and back onto Route 626.

Three miles away she skidded to a stop in the parking lot of Riverton Convenience Store. She jumped out, leaving the door swinging wide, and ran inside. Whitley trailed close behind after slamming the swinging door shut. A balding, stocky man of about sixty stood at the end of the counter, resting an elbow on an old-fashioned cash register while talking to an elderly man who was sitting in a rocking chair a couple yards away. The older man held a cane between his legs and a tin cup in one hand.

"What can I do for you, young lady?" the man who was standing asked, smiling as he turned to face Blair. Then, noticing her harried demeanor, he quickly inserted, "Is something wrong?"

"Yes . . . I . . . I don't know," she blurted, hyper-ventilating. "You see, I'm looking for someone . . . and . . . and . . ." Her voice stuttered to a stop, and she slumped against the counter.

"Here, drink this," the storekeeper said, pouring water into a paper cup from a bottle he had just taken from the refrigerator against the wall behind him. "It'll help you catch your breath."

As soon as she had taken several sips, he continued, "Now, tell me. What seems to have happened?"

Blair looked into his face and was instantly comforted. Deep blue eyes, framed by permanent laugh wrinkles, squinted softly, and a wide mouth smiled gently.

"I'm sorry, sir," Blair began, standing straighter, voice calmer, "I came in to ask if you had seen a woman this afternoon. She's about five-feet-four, has brown hair and eyes, is fortyish. Maybe she stopped here for something—"

"No. But I've been here just since 6:00," the man interrupted, then turned toward the other man, still sitting in the rocking chair. "Bim, you here all afternoon?"

"Yep. What was she driving, ma'am?" Bim asked, looking up at Blair, unhurriedly spitting into the tin cup he held, then wiping the back of his other hand across the three-day stubble around his mouth.

"Uh . . . uh . . . oh, hell, what's that car she just bought?" she asked herself, looking ceilingward and slapping her key case against her left palm. "Whitley, you know. What is it?" she asked, appealing to her son for help.

"A Suzuki Grand Vitara."

"Boys sure do know car models, that's certain," the storekeeper commented, wagging his head to indicate amazement for the ability.

"That one of them little short jobs with a tire on back?" Bim asked.

"Yes, sir," Whitley responded. Blair smiled at him proudly.

"Green?" Bim continued his questioning.

Whitley nodded affirmatively.

"Yep, I saw it. From the table back yonder," Bim said, jabbing his elbow in the direction of the rear section of the front window-wall and knocking his cane to the floor. "I heard Betty say 'A Pepsi? Is that all for you?' to a customer, but I didn't actually see who it was. Old Henry was sitting in front of me, blocking my line of sight."

"When was that, Mr. . . . uh, Bim? What time?" Blair asked, taking a step closer to him, as if her movement would hurry an answer. She picked up his cane and handed it to him.

"Not for sure exactly, ma'am. Thank you," he added, acknowledging her retrieval of his cane.

"I mean, at least approximately what time? Like maybe around 4:00—4:30?" Blair prompted.

"Ah, I see. Before that, though. I reckon a little before 3:00."

Blair's hopes plummeted. "And not again after that?" she pursued, holding her breath.

"No, ma'am. And I been here ever since then."

Blair exhaled wearily. Obviously Lauren had stopped at the store for a drink on her way *to* her appointment. This information was no help at all.

"Thank you. And thank you, too, sir," Blair added, addressing the storekeeper.

"I'm Hopkins Bryant, ma'am. Like I asked before, is something wrong? Is there anything I can do?"

Blair nodded. "Mr. Bryant, the woman is an agent with my company. She had an appointment to meet a customer at a listed property we have several miles east of here at 3:00. Her daughter says she hasn't returned nor phoned. I've been to the property. She's not there. I don't know what's happened . . . what to think—"

"Give me a number to call, in case I see her or hear anything," Hopkins Bryant directed. As Blair handed him her card, he added, "Meanwhile, try not to worry. She probably stopped somewhere to shop."

"I certainly hope you're right! Again, thank you. Good night."

Blair didn't speak again until she was driving out of the store parking lot. "Whitley, I'm going to take you home before I go to the office. If we don't locate Lauren soon, no telling how long I might be there," Blair said.

She phoned Richard. He had no news.

She phoned Page and updated her. "No news there either? Damn! Look, Page, I'm on my way home. I'll drop off Whitley and go on to the office. Meet me there at—well, in about forty-five minutes."

Whitley remained silent. Blair glanced at him. He was holding his Game Boy idly in his lap, his hands slack and his eyes apparently focused on the glove compartment latch directly in front of him.

"Are you okay, son?" she asked, putting her hand on his leg.

"Yeh . . . I s'pose. Mom, you think something bad has happened to Lauren, don't you?" he asked plaintively.

Blair patted his leg gently. "I don't know, Whitley. I really don't know what to think. Why do you say I think it's something bad?"

"Your voice back there. At the store. And your body language."

"A keen child, mine," Blair thought, again proudly. "I *am* worried, Whitley. It's not like Lauren to not contact

Page when she's going to be late getting home. But, as Mr. Bryant said back there, she may have gone shopping and simply lost track of time. Don't be upset. I'm sure we'll learn something soon."

Blair hoped that her verbal reassurances succeeded in making Whitley feel better. They surely weren't doing much for her.

TWO

At the office Blair quickly took control. One glance at Page told her that it was essential to assign the girl some tasks immediately. She was pale and noticeably nervous, standing zombie-like midway in the reception room.

"Richard packed sandwiches for us. You go get us drinks from the kitchen frig, ok?" Blair said. When the girl returned, Blair directed further, "Page, you man Lauren's desk. Let's make a list of the restaurants, stores, and shops in Lovingston and Amherst—maybe Scottsville, too—and look up their numbers. Then we'll divide the list and make calls."

It was now 9:15, according to Blair's watch. Businesses would be closing soon, some probably closed already. They had to hurry. Working from three phone books, in just a few minutes they had what they needed. Blair gave the Lovingston list to Page, aware that the girl was more familiar with local businesses, and picked up the Amherst and Scottsville lists to take to her own office.

"You use Line One, Page," she said over her shoulder as she crossed the reception room.

Thirty minutes later Blair emerged from her office. Page was sitting with shoulders hunched, staring at the remnants of her half-eaten sandwich. Even as she asked, Blair knew the answer to her question. "Any luck?"

"No," Page answered, quickly looking up at Blair, a tiny ray of hope flashing in her eyes. "You?"

"Nope. Sorry. Okay, it's time to call the sheriff's office . . ." Blair's voice trailed off as she picked up the phone in front of Page and dialed the number from memory.

Deputy Joe Brown and Investigator Ned Washburn arrived in five minutes flat.

"That *was* fast! Especially for this late hour," Blair said by way of greeting them at the front door, smiling her thanks.

"We were already at the office . . . working on a case . . ." Washburn returned, somewhat distractedly. "You said Lauren hadn't been seen since 2:00?" he asked, still not fully through the door.

"Two o'clock *here.* Three o'clock at Howardsville, according to a man at Riverton Convenience Store," Blair qualified. "This is Lauren's daughter, Page."

Both officers greeted Page, with an effort to be upbeat.

"I'll need that man's name later. Right now I need some other information," Washburn said as he took a seat at Lauren's desk and pulled a small spiral notebook from his inside jacket pocket. "First, Lauren's tag number."

"Page?" Blair queried, turning to the girl.

"I don't know . . . off-hand . . . but I can run home and look for something with the number . . . maybe a garage invoice or—"

"No, no, honey. No need to do that," Washburn interrupted. "Joe, get the number from DMV, will ya, then put out the APB."

Deputy Brown reached for Lauren's phone. Washburn stopped him, covering the phone with his hand. "Got another line, Blair?" he asked.

"Sure. Through that door over there, Joe. My office. Use Line Two," Blair instructed.

"Now," Washburn said, turning his attention back to Blair. "The name of the person Lauren was meeting today? Phone number, too, if you have it."

"The upper left drawer, please, if you'll open it. Should be a leather-bound appointment book in there. Thank you," Blair finished, as Washburn handed her the book.

Blair quickly turned to the page showing October 9. "Malcolm Earndahl from Fairfax," she read. "Here you go . . . his home number is right there," she pointed, handing the appointment book back to Washburn.

"Mind my calling long distance on this phone? My mobile is in another car," Washburn explained.

"No problem. Go ahead."

As he dialed the number, Blair turned away and walked to Page, who was standing behind a sofa, her hips pressing against its back.

"Damned stupid of me not to think of calling that number as soon as we got here!" Blair said, reprimanding herself.

"We couldn't think of everything," Page answered absently.

"I was just thinking of him being in *this* area, not back at his home—" Blair stopped short when she heard Washburn speaking.

"Yes, Mr. Earndul—oh, pronounced doll, is it? Sorry. Well, Mr. Earndoll, this is Ned Washburn with the Nelson County, Virginia sheriff's office. I understand you were scheduled to meet with Lauren Michaels of Town Mountain Realty this afternoon. Did you meet? You did. At what time? Uh-huh. Then what time did you leave the property? About 3:45, you say? Did Ms. Michaels leave ahead of you, or—oh, she was still there when you left. All right . . . hold a second, please," Washburn said, putting a hand over the mouthpiece when he realized Blair was tugging at his sleeve, trying to get his attention.

"What, Blair?"

"Ask him was anyone else at the property? If he saw anyone—any vehicle—parked nearby? Did Lauren mention having car problems? Or that she was going somewhere before returning to Lovingston? And also what kind of vehicle was he driving?"

Washburn frowned. Her rapid-fire questioning reminded him of the aggressiveness of her partner, Landis Galleher, during the previous year's murder investigation.

However, he nodded acknowledgment and asked Malcolm Earndahl all of her questions. Earndahl answered each negatively, then asked a question himself. "Why all these questions, you ask," Washburn resumed. "Well, sir, Ms. Michaels has not returned, and we're trying to locate her. Yes, that's right. Appreciate your help. Uh, give me your work number, please. Might need to contact you during daytime." Washburn added the number to his notes, thanked the man, and rang off.

"Did he know anything?" Page asked anxiously, approaching to lean over the desk front.

"Afraid not, Page. Said Lauren was still in the house when he left, turning off lights, locking up, doing whatever. And he was driving a Volvo sedan," Washburn directed to Blair. "When I get back to the office, I'll buzz the Fairfax police and ask them to check out Earndahl for me. Just a precaution, mind you."

Deputy Joe Brown returned to the reception room. "Got out the bulletin. Anything else we can do here?" he asked, directing the question to no one in particular.

"Don't think so," Washburn returned. "Blair, you and Page go on home. Joe and I will get on the horn to Dalton Savidge and start some action—"

"Who's Dalton Savidge? What action?" Blair interrupted.

"The new Emergency Services Director. He'll organize a search party. Joe's already got an all-points-bulletin out for Lauren's vehicle. Ya'll go on home now . . . try not to worry. I'll keep you posted on developments."

"Oh, all right!" Blair snapped, her last nerve almost showing. "Page, you going to be okay?" she inquired, looking sharply back at the girl.

"Yeah . . . I reckon," Page responded dejectedly.

"Tell you what. I'm gonna call your neighbor—your mom's friend Meredith—and ask her to stay with you. How's that?"

"Fine. Thank you."

"And call me anytime, you hear. Anytime at all," Blair insisted.

"I will. I promise." Page managed a weak smile of gratitude.

"Right, then. Settled," Washburn said. At the door he turned back, puzzlement showing on his face. "Where's the other one? Landis?"

"On a cruise, with . . . a friend." Blair caught herself before saying a name. No point announcing that the friend was Peter Mason—a figure from last year's murder investigation.

THREE

The sheriff's office was still abuzz with activity when Washburn and Brown returned at 11:00 p.m. The sheriff himself was there, along with two state troopers, six deputies, a dispatcher, and a secretary. In addition, a half-dozen people in jackets with "Rescue" emblazoned on the backs hustled about, talking on cell phones and jotting notes on their clipboards.

"Developments?" Washburn asked one of the rescue jackets, a bearded athletic six-footer in his mid-thirties.

"Nothing since you left," the man returned.

"Well, we got another."

"WHAT! You mean—"

"Indeed. Secretary-agent from out at Town Mountain Realty. Lauren Michaels. You know her, Jim?"

"Don't think so. Name's not familiar. Details?"

"She went to Howardsville—Albemarle County side—this afternoon to show a property to a guy from Fairfax. Not been seen since. Her daughter says she always phones."

"Howardsville . . . on the James River, too . . . east of where the other missing woman . . ." Jim mused. "Damn, Ned, you reckon—"

"That there's a connection?" Washburn finished for him. "Very possibly. Not obvious—at least not yet. One missing, you'd think it could be a car over a bank somewhere on those backroads. But *two* women gone missing no more than fifteen miles apart on the same day . . . I don't like what I'm thinking, Jim."

Jim Resdon nodded an understanding of Washburn's words. Jim was chief of the volunteer rescue group that worked under the direction of Dalton Savidge. In his eight years with the group he had never encountered a situation like this—two people reported missing the same day in the same general area, but under separate circumstances apparently.

"Did you ask this Lauren person's daughter if her mother knows Roberta Dumond?" Jim asked, seeking confirmation.

"No. Didn't even tell her that Mrs. Dumond is missing."

"Why?"

"The girl is scared enough already. Didn't see any point adding fuel tonight. Maybe we'll know more tomorrow. I'll tell Blair Camfield, Lauren Michaels's boss, then, too, and ask if they know Mrs. Dumond. And the other way around—ask Dumond's daughter if the Dumonds know Lauren," Washburn said, then asked, "Where's Dalton?"

"Took a crew to the Dumond house to relieve the first search team. This crew has dogs. Dalton's on the way back now. Just called in."

"Good. Though not for poor Dalton and you folks. Looks like we're all in for one helluva time! Well, I'd better check with dispatch. Maybe we'll get lucky with the APB. See you later," Washburn added as he walked away, wishing he could actually *believe* they would get a lucky break.

Four hours before Blair called the sheriff's office, Della Dumond Shales had called there to report her mother missing. Della's mother had picked Della up that morning to do grocery shopping together at IGA in Scottsville and then returned to Della's house. After eating a light lunch and copying Della's new recipe for crabcakes, Mrs. Dumond had left Della's to drive the six miles farther west to her own home. Widowed for ten years, Roberta Dumond lived alone in a large Colonial-style house with two dogs and a cat. She busied herself with extensive flower and vegetable gardens, church activities, two club memberships, varied volunteer services, and regular Thursday afternoon bridge parties. Called "Bert" by all her friends, she was well-liked and very popular in her end of the county. Thoughtful and predictable, she always notified Della or her good friend Antonia (Toni) Mathieson when there was to be a change in her usual routine.

So it was that Della had been somewhat concerned at first when her mother didn't answer her phone in mid-afternoon, more concerned an hour later when her mother, who had Caller ID, hadn't returned her call, and downright worried when she got no answer to her next attempted call at 4:45. Della hadn't tarried longer then. She had gotten her car from the garage and driven rapidly to her mother's house.

As she had turned into the driveway there, she had felt instant relief. Briefly. Her mother's Grand Cherokee was parked at the walkway leading to the back porch. "Mom must be in the garden gathering late veggies before frost," she had thought. But Mrs. Dumond had not been in the garden, not in the garage—and not in the house. With shaking fingers, Della had dialed a half dozen of her mother's friends. None had seen her or heard from her. Two had also tried phoning for hours, to no avail. All said that they would be right over.

Della had found nothing disturbed in the house. But two things were definitely disturbing. An unfinished thank-you note on her mother's desk and one dog missing. Alarm bells had sounded in her head at those two discoveries, prompting two panicky calls. One to the sheriff's office, one to her husband Winston.

Now Della and Winston Shales sat in her mother's family room, surrounded and attended to by members of her mother's church, the church where Roberta Dumond was chairperson of the Board of Trustees. *Some* of the church women present were her mother's friends.

"Did anyone check Roberta's Caller ID for stranger calls?" Marilyn Sodman asked as she sashayed into the house at 10:30.

"Of course, Marilyn! Early on. First Della did, then a sheriff's deputy," Toni Mathieson retorted, not trying to hide her annoyance at such an obvious question—and that being asked *five* hours after Bert's *friends* had arrived at her home! "There's coffee in the kitchen. Also plenty food if you want a snack," Toni added, relenting, good Southern manners taking command.

"Why, thank you, Antonia," Marilyn purred in a sugary tone. "Did you bring your special chicken salad?"

"No, I didn't!" Toni snapped, and walked across the room to avoid further communication.

Reva Harmon and Myra Corcoran exchanged glances and smiled. When Toni was beyond hearing distance, Reva said, "Bet Toni's blood pressure shot sky high from that encounter! Toni can't stand the rip."

"Even so, only Toni has the nerve to challenge her attitude."

"Her fakery, more precisely!" Reva scoffed.

"Whatever. Actually, I wonder why she bothers to come around us," Myra reflected.

"Huumph," Reva snorted, "she thinks we're her *impressed* audience! Poor fool."

The kitchen doorbell rang.

"Who's there?" Toni Mathieson called out.

"Dalton Savidge, with Emergency Services. I phoned here thirty minutes ago. Just need to introduce the dog handler who's heading up the relief search team."

Toni opened the door. Through the glass storm door she faced a tall dark-haired man sporting a crewcut and outfitted in camouflage. He smiled at her, revealing even, very white teeth. She unlatched the storm door. He opened it and walked in. Following on his heels was a shorter man, bearded, similarly camouflaged.

"You're Mrs. Mathieson, the person I spoke with?" Savidge asked. "The one in charge?" he added.

"Yes."

"Mrs. Mathieson, this is Eric Bonner. He and his crew will try to pick up a trail with dogs tonight. If they don't get a hit right off, they'll camp down and wait for daylight to fan out again. Can we have something with Mrs. Dumond's scent on it? Perhaps a piece of her clothing?"

"Surely. Myra, bring me Bert's sweater, will you?" Toni called out to the next room. "Mr. Savidge, Mr. Bonner, tell the searchers we'll have coffee and snacks here for them until—well, all night if necessary."

"Thank you, Mrs. Mathieson. That's most kind."

"Here's the sweater," Myra said, walking into the kitchen and holding the garment out to Toni. Dalton Savidge stepped forward and took it from Myra.

"Thank you," he said, smiling at her.

"Has the sheriff heard anything yet?" Myra asked.

"No. Not yet. Well, we'd better get on with it. Ya'll take care," Savidge said, nodding to both women. "Eric . . . ," he said, hand-motioning the dog handler to preceed him to the door.

Marilyn Sodman sidled into the kitchen as the door closed behind the two men.

"Who were they?" she asked, pointing to the closed door.

"Searchers."

"What happened exactly?" Marilyn asked, glancing from Myra to Toni. "I didn't want to ask back there in front of Della and Winston. And Jenny Brighton sure didn't give a very clear picture when she called to tell me! She was just plain hysterical."

"We know little more than what Jenny must have told you. That is, Bert left Della's house a little after 12:30; Della phoned her about 3:30; got no answer; called again at 4:45 and still got no answer. So she drove over here, found Bert's car at the back door but no Bert in the house and one dog missing. She looked in the gardens, the outbuildings, everywhere—to no avail. Then, as you know, she called all of us to find out if we knew where Bert was. Of course, you weren't home."

"You said 'little more'. What more? Has the sheriff's office learned anything? Any clues outside? Have Della and Winston—"

"Whoa, Marilyn! Hold on!" Toni commanded, overriding the onslaught. "We don't know *anything* other than what I just told you."

"Sorry. I just thought that perhaps the search parties . . . ," Marilyn said, beginning to defend herself, then trailed off.

"The first searchers, probably thirty or forty of them including the volunteers, covered Bert's property and a lot of the thousand acres of woodland behind but found nothing before they called off the search at dark. Now dog handlers are going out to see if they can pick up Bert's scent."

"Oh . . ." Marilyn fell silent for a moment, her brows knitted in a frown. "You think Bert just lost it and wandered off into the woods—"

"Dammit, Marilyn! Just shut the hell up!" Toni snapped, her hands balled into fists.

"Here, Marilyn, let me fix you a drink," Myra inserted quickly, hoping to diffuse the situation before a real scene erupted. She stepped behind the counter. "What would you like? Toni's just so upset! We all are."

"I'm outta here," Toni asserted, raising her hands and whipping them downward in a dismissive gesture as she turned and marched out of the kitchen.

FOUR

Thursday morning dawned crisp and clear, a perfect autumn harvest kind of day. At 6:15 Blair gave up the battle with sleeplessness. Sunrise found her sitting at the table in the breakfast room, a glass-walled area off the kitchen. Her first cup of coffee was becoming lukewarm as she stared out across the sprawling yard and to the farm pond beyond. The layer of wispy fog hovering over the water reminded her of cigarette smoke.

"Oh, damn!" she said aloud as she bumped her chair backward and stalked to the kitchen. "I've *got* to have a cigarette!"

Blair retrieved a full pack from a drawer in the small desk which she used mainly for recipe-writing and a phone base. She lighted the first cigarette she'd had in five days and took a deep drag. "Ah!" Her audible sigh expressed two-fold relief: for nicotine withdrawal and for the stress of Lauren's disappearance.

Exhaling a second time, she mumbled, "Oh, well . . . another abstinence shot to hell! Tough! It's smoking or gnawing fingernails. What a choice . . . die from emphysema or a perforated esophagus!"

"Talking to yourself, eh? Hope it helps. Especially more than that cig," Blair's husband said from the kitchen doorway.

Blair turned to face him, smiling faintly to cover her surprise. She had not heard him approaching. She looked down to his feet. No wonder she hadn't heard him . . . he was barefoot.

"You had trouble sleeping, too," she stated rather than asked. "Come on, I've got coffee brewed."

Blair poured Richard and herself cups of steaming coffee, heavily creaming hers. She popped bread into the double-toaster and retrieved a crock of her homemade cherry jam from the refrigerator. Back at the table in the breakfast room, they chatted about their sleeplessness and their concerns about Lauren.

"I'd like to go on to Lovingston in a few minutes," Blair concluded. "Need to e-mail Landis from the office. Need to meet with Washburn. Then need to organize whatever I can do to help . . ."

When her words trailed off, Richard glanced up, saw her woeful expression. "I can get the children off to school," he offered. "Call me at the office if there's news."

"I will, Rich," Blair murmured, near tears. "Thank you." She needed lots of support. His gesture provided a little.

She stood, touched his shoulder, and hurriedly left the room.

Blair arrived at her real estate office a few minutes before 7:30. First she checked voice mail. Nothing. Next she recorded a message for callers: "You have reached Town Mountain Realty. Due to an emergency, this office will be closed today. Please leave your name and number and a brief message. We'll contact you as soon as possible. Thank you." Then she hung a 9 x 12 poster displaying the same message on the front door, above the pocket-box which contained a notepad and pen.

Those chores done, she glanced at her watch. Probably a little too early, but it couldn't be postponed any longer. She plunked out a brief e-mail to Landis, ending it with "Don't do anything, especially don't interrupt your cruise, until you hear further from me. I mean it, Lan!" Looking toward Landis's office, she muttered, "But *how* I wish you were here!"

Time to call Washburn. She wasn't shocked to find him at the sheriff's office already.

"Anything, Ned?"

"Not really. Sorry." Washburn cleared his throat. "Blair, I need to talk to you. You at home?"

"No. The office."

"Good. Can you come over here? It's more convenient for me this morning."

"Sure. No problem. Be there in ten minutes." She was glad that he had invited her; it spared her having to ask—or beg—to get there. She needed desperately to be at the center of activity involved in the search for Lauren.

In the commons room at the sheriff's office, Washburn greeted Blair, poured two cups of coffee, and directed Blair to his private office at the end of a long narrow hallway.

"Cream? Sugar?" he asked as he moved a chair for her to one side of his desk.

"Cream, please. Lots."

From a small fiberglass table under a window he picked up two creamer packets and a stirrer for her. Then he sat down heavily in his desk chair, prompting Blair to look at him more keenly. His eyes were red-rimmed and his unshaved cheeks seemed to have deeper vertical creases, framing his nose in parentheses. The top button of his wrinkled shirt was undone and the knot of his tie was pulled down two or three inches.

"You've been here all night," Blair said, stating rather than asking.

"Up all night. Some time here, some riding with a deputy. Look bad, do I?" he grinned.

"No. Just haggard. I didn't sleep either, but I rested a little, I'm sure. And I did get a shower and change of clothes."

Washburn smiled ruefully. Then he looked down at a legal pad on his desk. "Fairfax police department reports that Earndahl is a respectable businessman with a nice family, no record, involved in community affairs, etc." he stated matter-of-factly, actually reading from his notes. He rolled a pen loosely between fingers and palm, silent as if lost in thought for a minute.

"Blair," Washburn began anew, lifting his head to look at her, then stopped talking to take a sip of coffee. Clearing his throat and idly tugging his tie, he continued, "Do you or Lauren know a woman named Roberta Dumond?"

"I do. She's a member of my church—in fact, chairman of the Board of Trustees. I don't think Lauren would know her, though. Why do you ask?"

"She's missing, too."

"WHAT!" Blair exclaimed, jumping up and nearly knocking over the coffee cup she had placed on a corner of Washburn's desk.

Washburn rose swiftly and caught her arm. Their eyes locked. They stood close together. Longer than necessary for him to steady her balance. Then he gently steered her back into her chair.

"Wha . . . what happened? When?" she asked tremulously, trying hard to sound calmer than she felt.

"Yesterday afternoon. Disappeared from her house."

"Did you know this when I phoned about Lauren last night?"

"Yes."

"And didn't tell me!" Blair shouted shrilly.

"Blair, hold on! Listen a minute! I thought it best not to alarm you. Or Lauren's daughter. Especially considering we didn't know—still don't know—if there's a connection. But it *is* a strange coincidence . . . two women disappearing in the same general area, maybe less than fifteen miles apart, so close to the same time—"

"You're damned right!" Blair blurted. "Have you checked the list of registered sex offenders and ex-convicts in the area?" she demanded.

"Of course we have! There's no one on the list in a thirty-mile radius. But we're questioning some in Charlottesville. Look, I have deputies canvassing a forty-mile stretch along the James River, going east and west of the points of the women's disappearances. Somebody will turn up a lead. And pretty soon, I think! Now, back to my asking you to come here. First, I wanted to tell you about Mrs. Dumond; second, I want to call Lauren's customer—Earndahl—with you present; third, would you like to ride with me to your listed property in Albemarle? Already got Albemarle deputies and some of ours there—"

"Yes, absolutely!" Blair responded unhesitatingly. Her palms were damp, her forearms goose-bumpy. She left her chair and began pacing back and forth between desk and window.

Washburn watched her for a few seconds, thinking—despite himself and the situation—how very attractive she was. And vulnerable at the moment. He decided not to mention to her a possibility that had crossed his mind: that maybe Blair, not Lauren, had been the intended second victim—if indeed there was a church connection. He struggled to resist the urge to get up and put his arms around her. Instead, he turned to his phone and dialed Earndahl at his office in Fairfax.

"Earndahl, Ned Washburn with Nelson County sheriff's office again. Another question. Did Lauren Michaels, the real estate agent, show you the inside of any of the farm buildings yesterday afternoon? No? Do you know why . . . did she say? Oh, sure, I understand. Makes sense. Just a sec . . . Ms. Michaels' boss has a question for you."

Washburn cupped the mouthpiece with his left hand. "He says he wasn't interested in the property after seeing the area and the house, so there was no point looking at the other buildings. What's your question?"

Blair reached for the receiver, blurting instead, "Let me talk to him." Washburn frowned, but handed her the phone nevertheless.

"Mr. Earndahl, this is Blair Camfied, co-owner of Town Mountain Realty. I want you to know that we appreciate your interest in this area of Virginia, that we're genuinely sorry you've been caught up in the investigation of Ms. Michaels' disappearance, and that we wish you a more successful real estate experience next time around. We'll certainly keep your interests in mind. Just one more question, if you don't mind. Did Ms. Michaels seem upset, aggitated, distracted in any way?"

Blair listened for a minute, then finished, "Yes, that's very helpful. Thank you. Of course, we'll keep in touch. 'Bye for now."

Washburn had observed her with interest during the call. Now he looked away for a second and grinned. "What a consummate sales person!" he thought. He couldn't help admiring her touch.

"Well?" he queried when she didn't speak immediately. "What did he say?"

"That Lauren was cheerful, laughed at his jokes, and certainly appeared well and happy. Also said he was impressed with her friendliness and sales approach."

That was no surprise to Washburn—not with Blair as her mentor. "Why did you say 'that's very helpful'?" he asked.

"What he said suggests that she wasn't *aware* of any problem or any danger, that she wasn't afraid."

"What's your point, Blair?"

"That whoever is involved in her disappearance is likely *not* someone she knows, so we don't need to use up valuable investigative time chasing—"

"Hey, hold on! First of all, *I* decide the direction of the investigation. Second, what's with the 'we'?" Washburn demanded.

"Well . . . I mean . . . LOOK, I *am* involved. Lauren is my friend and my employee. I'm not about to sit still and do nothing!" Blair retorted.

"Blair, I understand your feelings, but let's be clear here. We'll involve you as warranted, and we'll certainly keep you informed about developments, but you simply cannot get into this independently."

"Why not?"

"Because if you go off half-cocked you can get hurt!" Washburn returned passionately. Realizing belatedly that he had revealed a profound personal concern, and in an attempt to dilute it, he quickly added, "Besides, you might obstruct the official investigation."

"I won't interfere or obstruct. You know how Landis and I helped with last year's murder investigation—"

"How well I remember! But still . . . oh, all right. But, at least, will you promise to check with me before you act and that you won't confront anybody when you're alone?"

Genuine concern echoed in his last words—and something more. She looked at him, saw the gravity of his expression—and relented.

"Yes, Ned, I promise. I won't do anything utterly stupid. Now, can we go to the property? After I phone Page?"

"Sure. And after I get a quick shower in the locker room."

Twenty minutes later he reappeared—clean, shaved, and sporting a fresh shirt and tie.

FIVE

As they entered the Bannister property, Blair counted six sheriff's department cars, three from Nelson and three from Albemarle County, along with one state police car and one emergency services panel truck. Crime-scene tape stretched across the front yard and along both sides of the driveway. A group of people, perhaps as many as fifty, stood beside the tape on the east side of the driveway. Two deputies stood in front of them talking earnestly, judging from the gesticulating of their hands and arms.

Washburn pulled over and rolled down his window. "What's going on there, Joe? Problem?" he asked.

"Naw. Just local people. Albemarle Deputy Howard and I are interviewing 'em for search parties. Already done another group. Some of these here are familiar with the area back there," Deputy Brown answered, pointing to the two-thousand-acre expanse of forest behind the Bannister lot. "Savidge's crews're stretched pretty thin . . . with the other situation and all . . ." he trailed off.

Washburn nodded. "Sure. We need all the help we can find. Good work. Get on with it."

At the house parking area, Washburn introduced Blair to a state trooper, Albemarle's chief investigator, two Nelson deputies, and two emergency services crewmen.

"How do we want to work this, Dave?" Washburn addressed David Phelps, the Albemarle investigator. "We got the missing person, you got the territory," he elaborated.

"Yeah. What say we divide the task here? One county take the house, driveway, and immediate yard area—the other take the rest of the lot and the outbuildings. Your choice?"

"My deputies and I'll take the lot and outbuildings," Washburn responded.

"Fine. Let's get back together in about an hour to combine notes, okay?"

"Sure."

"Come on, boys," Phelps called to the two Albemarle deputies. "We'll start with the house."

Washburn turned back to the two men standing beside their cars. "Seen anything already, Orie?" he asked, addressing a tall black deputy whom he had introduced to Blair as Orieman Taskell.

"Maybe so, sir. Something down there I want to show you," he said, pointing toward the lower backyard.

"Hank, you go walk the lot border all the way around, okay? Look for anything disturbed," Washburn directed.

Deputy Taskell walked Washburn and Blair to the shed which the evening before Blair had considered a storage area for garden tools and lawnmowers. Its door was still partly open.

"Is this how you found it?" Washburn asked, pointing to the door as they approached.

"Yes. And none of us stepped inside yet, either. Wanted you to take a look first. See those two marks in the dust—trailing three feet or so in from the doorway, looks like?" the deputy finished, motioning for Washburn to approach the open door.

"Or, more likely, trailing from three feet inside *back* to the door," Washburn suggested, noting no disturbance in the dust beyond the three-foot point.

"Right, sir, that's what I meant," Taskell qualified, apologetically.

"You go in there last night, Blair?"

"No. Just looked in."

"Orie, go get your stuff and bring it down here. Might be something to print on the door latch. Even inside. Blair, stay back while I go in, okay?"

Blair nodded assent.

Washburn donned plastic gloves and stepped through the doorway to the left of the lines in the dust. He removed his sunglasses and squinted to adjust to the semi-darkness. In a few seconds he could discern footprints leading from the right side of the doorway. They revealed a distinct tread design.

"Blair," he called, "tell Deputy Taskell to bring a camera, too."

He squatted beside the point of origin of the skid marks. "Ah!" he exclaimed. Just in front of the right skid, and partially turned outward, was the print of a *smooth* shoe sole.

"Blair, come to the door," he called. She poked her head in, her hands pressed firmly on her knees to avoid touching anything.

Washburn smiled. Her amateurish sleuthing technique *was* rather charming, he had to acknowledge privately. "What kind of shoes was Lauren wearing yesterday?" he asked.

"Uh . . . let me think . . . had on slacks, not jeans . . . so black flat pumps, I'm pretty sure."

"Leather soles?"

"I guess. I don't know. Why?"

"There's a smooth-soled shoe print here," he said, pointing with a forefinger, "with what appears to be a flat heel. And over there, coming this way, appear to be shoe prints with a very distinct design of some sort."

Blair shuddered. "You think . . . Lauren was in here . . . and someone else—"

"Not sure," he interrupted, to divert her thinking. "Don't draw any—"

"Excuse me," Deputy Taskell said to Blair, startling Washburn and her. "Here's the camera."

"Hand it in to me, please," Washburn directed.

Washburn took numerous close-up shots of the footprints and skid marks, then carefully skirted them to reach the door. From outside he took several wide shots of the interior.

"Orie, dust this hasp latch, the wood panel next to it, and then the door frame here—above and below the hook fastener. Don't go inside. We'll leave that for the Albemarle CS guys. Get Joe down here to tape off the whole building. Wait! Looks like he'll still be busy with the searchers. I'll get Hank to do it."

Washburn put two fingers in his mouth and with a sharp whistle signaled Hank Parker. "Tape needed down here, Hank!" he yelled.

He looked around to say something to Blair. She was nowhere in sight. He walked to the right side of the storage building. No Blair. Around back he found her. She was on her knees, gingerly stirring a small area on the ground with a six-inch stick.

"*What* exactly are you doing?" he asked, more stridently than he intended.

"Ned! Walk a little more away from the wall—over here behind me. Want you to look at this."

Blair had removed bits of brownish grass away from a footprint, now clearly outlined in damp red soil. "Is this design like what you saw inside?"

Washburn leaned over her shoulder and peered at the ground. "Looks to be. See any more of them?"

"Not this distinct. But there is something else." She stood abruptly, bumping hard against his chest and shoulders. She turned in order to straighten fully, and for seconds they stood very close together facing each other. Their eyes locked and held. Washburn was the first to react, stepping back from her.

"Huum-ump," Blair cleared her throat as she turned her back to him, obviously rattled. Neither could deny the chemistry generated between them. "Damn," she thought, "I don't need *this*! And certainly not now!"

Washburn broke the silence. "There was something else?"

"Yes," Blair responded quickly, grateful for a return to business. "Look at these two flattened lines in the grass coming around the left corner. Tire tracks, I think."

"Sure thing! Hey, you got a good eye!" Washburn exclaimed, excited, and without reservation. "Okay . . . so looks like someone pulled a vehicle around here to hide it . . . maybe when hearing Lauren and/or her customer pulling into the gravel driveway from the highway. The slope of the yard would have prevented them from seeing a vehicle down here until they were right up to the house—actually not until they got around to the back of the house. By then someone could have secluded a vehicle back here."

Blair picked up the scenario. "Then this person slipped inside the shed to wait until they left. But why was he here in the first place . . . why the need to hide . . . and what could have brought Lauren down here if the customer didn't want to see the outbuildings?" she mused. "Wait! You think maybe Earndahl could be lying? Maybe he *was* the one waiting down here for Lauren to arrive?"

Washburn shook his head. "No. Why here? If he had an intention to do Lauren harm, why wouldn't he have just waited up at the house? It's vacant."

"Well . . . true. Then, too, there's the other . . . Roberta Dumond. Earndahl couldn't have known where she lived. And I *do* think there's a connection!"

"Very possible," Washburn agreed.

"Ned, look more closely at these tire tracks. What size tires made them, do you think?"

He smiled at her, conveying acknowledgment, and appreciation, of her keen observation skill. "Larger than sedan size, like the 205/75 R15's on my car, that have a tread width approximately seven inches. Let's see." Washburn removed a small tape measure from a belt pouch and knelt to measure the tire imprint. "Ten-point-seven," he announced, returning the tape measure to its pouch and writing the measurement in his mini-notebook.

"What'dya think? A pick-up truck?"

"Maybe. Or maybe some model or other of SUV. Stand back a little, will 'ya? Let me get a picture of each print from this angle."

Washburn snapped several camera shots of the tire marks. "Let's see if Orie's found anything," he directed when he had finished his camera work. Blair caught the "Let's" and smiled at his casual inclusion of her in the investigative activity. It was reminiscent of Landis and her working with Washburn in the previous year's open-house murder investigation—and underscored her wishing that Landis were here now.

Deputy Taskell had dusted two fingerprints on the flat door latch. "Think this'll be the best I can get. Couldn't pick up anything on the wood surfaces," he reported.

"Good work, Orie. Hank, you find anything?" Washburn asked the other deputy, standing near Deputy Taskell and holding a roll of yellow tape.

"Nothing," the genial-faced, stocky deputy answered.

"So, okay, you can tie off now, Hank. We're finished with this building for the time being. We'll move on to the other buildings, unless you're scheduled to go with the searchers. Are you?"

"Well . . . uh, yeah. An Albemarle deputy and I are taking out a party of twelve. Joe and another guy are heading up the other group." Deputy Hank Parker glanced at his watch. "We'll get going as soon as the two emergency services volunteers up there are ready. Should be in about ten minutes. Orie, Trooper Derek, and Investigator Phelps are gonna continue working this scene with you, right?"

"Right. See you later. Good luck."

Deputy Parker nodded an acknowledgment, then began tying off the perimeter with yellow tape.

"Washburn!" Blair called out. She was down on her knees again, this time beside an anthill located about eight feet from the shed door. The anthill had been a small pile of red dirt, about three inches in diameter. Now it was mashed flat. Washburn squatted beside Blair. "Does this heel mark look like the one you saw inside?" she asked, turning toward him—and finding his face only inches from hers. She quickly averted her gaze to the anthill.

He squinted, then twisted sideways to look at the print from a different angle. "Pretty much, I think," he said, whipping up the camera and snapping a couple shots. Then he stood, bent low as he stepped forward to scan the ground around the area. Dead grass extended thirty feet outward from the shed, obscuring evidence of any other prints there. He moved uphill for sixty feet or so to a spot of bare ground.

"Blair . . . Orie . . . here're tire marks! Same width as those behind the shed—probably heading to the highway."

Catching up to Washburn, Blair glanced at the tire marks, then looked back at the shed. Left hand on hip, right forefinger pressed to her cheek, she began to speculate. "He dragged Lauren out of the shed, dragged or carried her to the vehicle after it was brought back around front, touched her foot down on that anthill as he was loading her in, then drove off." Suddenly she cupped her face in her hands. "To God knows where!" she muttered brokenly.

No one said anything for the next minute or two, each mentally forming a scenario. Blair chose to picture the heel print on the anthill as evidence that Lauren had possibly stood upright, thus suggesting that she *could have* left the property alive.

"But where's her car?" she blurted loudly, breaking the silence.

"Could have been more than one person involved, Blair. And took her car with them," Washburn offered. "Look, I know you're upset. Why don't you go sit in my car for—"

"NO!" she cut him off emphatically. "I'm staying with it! Really, I'm okay. I *need* to stay involved for Lauren's sake."

"All right. Come on, let's take a look at the barns," Washburn conceded. "The guys can cast molds of the tire track and footprint later."

The building which Blair had designated a cow barn the evening before had a twenty-foot platform on the left front and a cattle-loading chute running fully along the left side. A wide door at front center led into a passageway, or corridor. To both sides of the corridor were stalls, and at the far end a stairway led to the hayloft. The floor was littered with loose particles of old hay, corncobs, a rope, two badly dented buckets, and numerous empty feed bags. Cobwebs hung from the ceiling nearly to the floor. It was obvious that no one had been inside the barn for a long time.

When they were back outside, Blair veered away from the men, jumped up on the platform—and simultaneously expelled a blood-curdling scream. Washburn and Taskell whirled around in time to see Blair running across the long platform at full throttle—then her tennis-shoe shod feet bicycling through space for another twelve feet! They were still gaping when she hit the ground, rolled into a ball, and attempted to jump up. Then they both doubled over, guffawing loudly.

"Dammit to hell, don't just stand there! Laughing like hyenas!" she snapped.

Washburn moved first. When he reached her, he extended his hand to help her up. "What happened?" he asked, still chuckling.

She swatted his hand away—angry, embarrassed, hurting.

"What—" he began to ask again.

"A g.d. SNAKE! Right up there," she hissed, pointing back to the platform. Now in a sitting position with her left leg drawn back and chin resting on the knee, she was rubbing the left ankle.

Deputy Taskell went to the platform. "Sure enough, Captain, it IS!" he called over his shoulder. "A big devil, too—just stretched out sunning hisself! As easy as you please. Want me to kill him?"

"No, no. Leave it. Not hurting anyone. Well, not *now* anyway," Washburn answered, tongue-in-cheek. Turning back to Blair, he asked, "Are you hurt?"

"I don't know . . . yes, a little. Think I did something to my left ankle when I jumped the snake. Snakes panic me to death!"

He knelt and examined the ankle, his hand warm and caressing on her calf as he held the foot with his other hand and gently rotated it left to right.

Blair winced from pain, but she held back a scream. Only a barely audible "Ow-oh" escaped her lips as tears welled in her eyes.

"Don't think it's broken," Washburn pronounced, "but surely a bad sprain. Come here, Orie. Let's get her up and see if she can stand."

They reached down, each placing a forearm in one of her armpits, and hoisted her with little effort.

"Put your weight on the left," Washburn directed.

Blair leaned to her left, winced, and immediately lurched the other way. Hard against Washburn.

"Orie, go bring my car down here, will you?"

"Sure thing," Taskell responded, already going uphill at a running walk.

Blair was painfully conscious of Washburn's closeness, of his forearm pressing her ribcage near her right breast. As if suddenly aware that she might be discomforted, he moved his arm from under hers and placed a hand under her elbow.

To lighten the tension between them, he spoke. "That really was a funny sight, Blair—your little feet pawing air like a puppy swimming upstream! We couldn't help laughing. Shoot, I'll picture it mentally for years, I know."

"And laugh like hell every time, I'm sure! But it's okay. I know I must have looked pretty silly."

"Well . . ." he said, grinning a little. "Of course, we didn't know you were hurt. We wouldn't have laughed if—"

"I know," she said, conceding. And smiled at him.

Deputy Taskell pulled the car as close to Blair as he could, jumped out, and hurried around the passenger side to help Washburn. He opened the rear door, automatically from habit.

When they had gotten her seated and the door closed, she lowered the window part-way. "So, now I'm to experience a prisoner's ride, huh?" she joked.

Chuckling, Washburn handed Taskell a five-dollar bill. "Go back there to Riverton Store, buy some ice for her ankle. Maybe liniment, too. Then let her rest in the car until we finish here."

Less than an hour later the search party with Deputy Joe Brown found Lauren's mini-SUV. Two searchers returned to the crime-scene yard to report the find to Washburn and Investigator Phelps, while the others continued their search into the forest for Lauren.

Washburn and the state trooper followed the two searchers to Lauren's vehicle. It was parked a hundred feet off an old wagon trail in the woods about a quarter mile from the barns. Someone had driven the Suzuki over waist-high undergrowth to where it was found off trail. Its green color had helped to camouflage it.

Their peripheral examination revealed no apparent damage to the vehicle and no blood or other evidence of injury to Lauren. Her pocketbook, cell phone, and a manila folder rested on the front passenger seat. The folder was labeled "Bannister Property". With gloved hands, Washburn opened the driver's door. He examined the contents of pocketbook and folder. The wallet contained a driver's license, pictures, business cards, three credit cards, and forty-four dollars in cash. The manila folder contained a plat, a copy of the Bannister listing agreement, a disclosure statement, some hand-written notes, and a page with information on Earndahl's real estate needs. Nothing in the vehicle seemed disturbed in any way; rather, it appeared to be just the way Lauren would have left it as she stepped out. That very fact was puzzling. The items resting on the passenger seat suggested that only one person had been in the vehicle when it was hidden in the woods. What person?

Trooper Derek phoned for a roll-back wrecker truck to pick up the Suzuki and take it to the sheriff's office lot, where a forensics team would go over it in detail for fingerprints and other evidence.

After their conference was completed and details for continuing investigative efforts were discussed, Washburn and Phelps shook hands and said good-bye. Trooper Derek returned to highway patrol tasks. Deputy

Orieman Taskell remained at the scene to coordinate communication among the searchers and Albemarle deputies, while Washburn left to drive Blair back to Lovingston.

SIX

"So, what d'ya think happened?" Blair asked when Washburn finished describing for her the discovery and initial examination of Lauren's vehicle. They were just entering the highway from the Bannister property driveway.

"Looks like Lauren surprised at least one person who was here for something he, or they, wanted to keep secret. Made Lauren drive the Suzuki into the woods—if she was conscious—or drove it there himself if—"

"Conscious?" Blair interrupted. "Then you think that she *is* alive?" she continued, voice somewhat brightened by hope.

"Well . . . yes . . . possibly. At least *was*. Otherwise, likely we would have found her body at the shed or near her SUV."

"Oh," Blair said, her voice reflecting some diminishment of hope.

"Blair, don't give up. You said yourself that Lauren is strong, resourceful—"

"Yeah, but not if she was slugged from behind, not if—"

"LOOK," he interrupted decisively, "let's focus on something else. Lauren's contacts. Has she had a run-in with anyone lately? Is there someone whose advances she rejected? Anyone jealous of—"

"Hey! I just remembered something. She was calling her ex-husband earlier this week. Something about dental work and tuition for Page."

"Which day this week?"

"Tuesday, I think. Yes, Tuesday. I remember for sure."

"What's his name?"

"Rudolph Michaels. Rudy."

"Lives in Nelson?"

"No. Staunton. I'm pretty sure his address and phone number are in Lauren's desk directory. But if not, Page would know."

"Good. I'll check him out. Who else comes to mind—anybody we might consider?"

"Uh . . . let me think. Maybe Lew Groveland."

"Who's he?"

"A part-time agent we had. Landis fired him about two weeks or so ago."

"Why?"

"An argument with Lauren. Actually, he argued or complained all the time about something. Not getting a fair share of leads, he felt. Not getting enough commission split. Not getting the floor-duty days he wanted. That kind of thing."

"Blair! To the point. What was his argument with Lauren about?"

"Accused her of stealing a customer of his and making a sale. Said he was due the commission."

"Was it true?"

"Of course NOT!"

"Why did he think so?"

"Okay. See, we have a written floor-duty policy. There's a schedule of agent assignments, by date. The main feature of it is that walk-in customers go to the agent with floor duty that particular day. Lew often asked to switch days with someone. The day in question he had switched days with Lauren. An investor-type guy walked in, hit if off with Lauren, and spent the day looking at four or five properties. He made offers on two of them. The offers were accepted by the sellers and settlement is scheduled for November 1. Lew contended that because the day was originally assigned to him, the customer was meant to be his and that he should get the commissions—or half, at the least."

"He confronted Lauren at the office?"

"No. Called her at home at night. Then she called Landis. The next morning Landis and I met with both of them at the office. Landis reminded him of the floor-duty policy, reiterating that his voluntarily switching days with Lauren officially rotated his assignment day to what had been Lauren's day. Well, he just exploded! Went off big time—yelled a few things at us, called Lauren a few names. And that did it! Landis ordered him to pack his things and get out right then. Later that day she wrote him a letter of termination and returned his license to the Real Estate Board at Virginia's Department of Professional and Occupational Regulation in Richmond."

"Any of you heard from him since?"

"Not directly. Heard he had made some remarks around town."

"Like what?"

"Oh, stuff like he was going to report us to the Board, see that we lost our licenses, going to sue the company, etc."

"But he hasn't?"

"Nope. Hasn't a leg to stand on! Just venting."

"Maybe. Know where I can contact him?"

"Used to have a Faber address, but I heard an agent in Charlottesville say that he had moved there."

"By the way, how much commission money are you talking about?"

Blair closed her eyes, mentally calculating percentages. "Lauren's split, close to $50,000."

"Huumm . . . interesting," Washburn mused, as he digested the information. "Okay. Anyone else?"

"Maybe Derek Tanner."

"The town wine-o? Why him, for heaven's sake?"

"I didn't say him for sure, Ned! It's just that he made remarks to Lauren whenever he saw her on the street."

"You mean like the remarks we've run him in at least a hundred times for making? Remarks to every female he passes?"

"Well . . . yeah. But one day there could be fire where there had only been smoke before!"

"Okay, okay. I'll question him. Who else?"

"I can't think of anyone else . . . wait. She did have two male customers last week—came in together—but she would have said something to me if there had been anything out of line about them."

"Names?"

"I don't know. I'll have to check her calendar."

"Right. Just call the info to me when you get to your office, okay? Then you need to run on by Blue Ridge Medical and get that ankle checked."

"Boy, I don't need reminding! It's hurting like hell."

"How about my sending someone along to help you in and out—"

"Thanks. But no. I can manage just fine."

"Okay, whatever you say," he said as they drove into the parking lot at the sheriff's office. "At least, I'll help you into your car."

Washburn parked beside Blair's sedan, passenger side to her driver's side. "Stay in your seat until I get around there to open your door," he directed.

Blair allowed him to assist her, but made no further comment—even when she felt disturbed by the pressure of his hands on her waist as he supported her movement across the short distance to her driver's seat. She gave him a small cupped-hand wave as she reversed from the parking spot. From her rear-view mirror she observed that he stood for a moment, watching her retreating vehicle, before turning away and walking toward the sheriff's office entrance.

"Damn," she muttered. She realized there was no getting around the fact that she had a problem. Serious one, too. She and Ned Washburn definitely felt an attraction—actually a rather intense chemistry. Divorced, he could afford it. Happily married with two children, she couldn't. Well, maybe not *absolutely* happily. But, still, she couldn't . . . just couldn't. "Well, at least not right now," a little inner voice taunted. And she hated the stress she was feeling, knowing she would have to address the issue. Soon, too. She would have to get it out in the open, actually have to kill the feelings with words. To Ned.

Once again she wished that Landis were in town. Talking to her about it would help alleviate the pressure.

For sure the bluntly frank Landis would have a suggestion about how to handle the situation—no doubt with humor thrown in!

"Oh well, 'I'll think about that tomorrow!' as Scarlet would say," Blair said to her empty car. She reached for her cell phone, stopped in front of the post office, and dialed Lauren's daughter to report on the discoveries at the Bannister property that morning.

She stopped by her real estate office to look up the names of Lauren's two male customers from the previous week. She phoned the sheriff's office and gave the names to the secretary-receptionist, asking that she pass the information on to Washburn. Then she paid a brief visit to the medical center. A nurse-practitioner wrapped her ankle tightly, gave her some sample pain pills, lent her a pair of crutches, and instructed her to keep her weight off the foot for several days.

"Never happen!" she muttered on the way home, recalling the nurse's admonition. "Five dogs to be fed and walked; two children to be fed, clothed, and driven to a dozen activities; one dull, lazy husband to be catered to . . . Whoa, Blair! Cool it!"

Blair never talked about her husband Richard to friends and acquaintances. Most of them hardly knew him. Those who did know him regarded him as a decent, pleasant man—but somewhat reserved. Typical accountant, they probably thought. Blair agreed with their assessment. However, only she could add qualifications. Very quickly into their twelve-year marriage, she had learned that the quietness in Richard translated as a certain lack of social interests, lack of intellectual curiosity, lack of *flair* and sense of adventure. He was a good father and a faithful husband. Over the years, with two children, they had developed a "comfortable" lifestyle, and Blair was devoted to her family. But the stylishly attractive, witty, energetic, people-oriented Blair found the relationship with Richard not very challenging or rewarding. Not even very interesting. Thus she was finding herself somewhat vulnerable to the attentions of a handsome, witty, risk-taking man like Ned Washburn—a take-command, decisive man who was also sensitive and sensual.

When Blair reached home at 3:00 no one was there. Whitley and Meade would get off the school bus at 4:00, and Richard would arrive a few minutes after 5:00 if he didn't have a late appointment. She parked close to the back door and managed to hop into the house on the crutches with little trouble. After hugging and petting the dog menagerie and preparing herself a late lunch, she settled into a recliner in the den. Almost immediately she looked up Roberta Dumond's number and dialed. On the third ring a woman answered.

"Mrs. Shales?" Blair asked.

"No. This is Toni Mathieson. How may I help you?"

"Oh, hi Toni. This is Blair Camfield. Is Bert's daughter there? Is it possible for me to speak to her?"

"Of course, Blair. How are you these days?"

"I'm fine. No, actually I'm not. But, really, I can't go into that now, Toni." Blair knew Toni well enough to be so blunt. In fact, Toni would understand readily. They were similar personalities.

"Sure. Just a minute. I'll tell Della you're on the line. Talk to you later."

"Yes? This is Della," a husky voice came through a minute later.

"Della, this is Blair Camfield, a member of your mother's church. I just heard about Bert's disappearance today. That's why I hadn't phoned earlier. Sorry."

"I understand. I'm glad to hear from you. Mother speaks of you often—with fondness and respect."

"I'm very fond of her, too. She's a lovely lady. Uh . . . Della, I know you're devastated . . . know you're under a great deal of pressure . . . but I need to discuss . . . actually need to ask you some questions. Is this an appropriate time, or should I call some other time?"

"Now is all right, Blair. Some of the church women are taking care of everything here. And I could use a time-out."

"Well, I'm afraid what I have to say will be anything but a pleasant time-out. An agent from my office, Lauren Michaels, disappeared yesterday afternoon, too. From a property three miles east of Howardsville. And I was wondering—"

"WHAT! For God's sake! You mean, just disappeared like my mother?" Della shrieked.

"Yes."

"Well, it's certainly odd that none of the deputies or searchers mentioned it yesterday . . . last night!"

"They didn't know it then, Della. An investigator is going to talk to you today, just like he waited until today to tell me about your mother . . . about Bert. Deputies are interviewing people up and down the river today, trying to find out if there's a connection. It's what I'm wondering, too. Do you know if Bert knows Lauren Michaels?"

"I've never heard her mention the name. Does Ms. Michaels live down here on the river?"

"No. She lives a few miles west of Lovingston. Forty-ish, divorced, mother of three. Goes to a Baptist church somewhere in that end of the county, I think."

"With the age difference and the other—rather, the different denomination I mean—I doubt if Mother knows her," Della ventured.

"I doubt it, too. I've never heard Lauren say she knows anyone down this way—other than my family, of course."

"What was she doing near Howardsville? Tell me the details. Maybe something will reveal a clue."

"Okay. She left the real estate office yesterday a few minutes after 2:00 to go to show a property on Route 626 in Albemarle at 3:00. According to a customer at Riverton Convenience Store, Lauren stopped there to get a drink a few minutes before 3:00. She met her customer, a man from Fairfax, at 3:00 and showed him the house. It didn't suit his needs. He said that he left at 3:45 and that Lauren remained behind to cut off lights and lock-up. When her daughter phoned me at 6:30 to say that Lauren had not come home, I drove to the property, found nothing, and returned to the office to call stores, restaurants, etc. where she might have gone. No luck. No one has seen or heard from her since. Searchers found her vehicle this morning—in the woods about a fourth of a mile from the listed house. And we found some drag marks and footprints in and around a shed—"

"WE?" Della interrupted, sounding incredulous.

"I went back to the property this morning. With Investigator Washburn. I'm trying to help—"

"God, I wish *I* could do something, too! I just don't know what . . ." Della trailed off.

"What time did your mother disappear? Washburn might have told me, but . . ."

"Not sure. But definitely sometime between 1:00 and 3:30. She left my house at 12:45, would have gotten to her house by 1:00. I phoned her at 3:30 and got no answer . . . and, of course, no answer to my next call at 4:45. At that time I drove here, found her gone, her Jeep in the driveway, a partially written note on her desk, and one of her dogs missing."

"Huumm . . . Bert gone no more than two hours before Lauren and a dozen or so miles apart . . . Della, did the deputies find tire tread marks in Bert's driveway, different from her tire treads?"

"I don't think so. They didn't say. But the driveway is paved."

"Yeah, that's right. I forgot. I'll check with Washburn anyway. If they don't have anything, would you mind if I come down this afternoon and have a look-about?"

"Well . . . I mean, sure. Can't hurt. I'll help you."

"Thanks. See you about 4:00, then. And, Della, think positive. It's not finished. We're gonna find them!"

"I hope so, Blair. Thank you. 'Bye," Della said, voice breaking.

They hung up. "Hot damn!" Blair exclaimed, slapping her thigh. "Ouch," she squeaked when pain shot through her ankle. When the pain subsided, she hoisted herself to the crutches. "Get the Polaroid," she went on talking aloud, "and pray there's film left in it." If Della should ask, she would pretend she'd called Washburn.

For the third or fourth time, she wished again that Landis were home to go sleuthing with her.

SEVEN

Ned Washburn met with searchers and deputies Friday morning at 8:00 in the conference room at the sheriff's office.

"All right . . . listen up," he called out, in raised voice to settle the group to attention. When they were seated and more or less quiet, he picked up a sheaf of papers and a legal pad and stepped to the front of the group.

"I've read your interview reports," he said, holding up the sheaf of papers and waving it slightly. "And I appreciate all the hard work you've done during the past forty hours. In summary, however, looks like all we got so far is one person who saw a dark-colored van or SUV leaving Mrs. Dumond's driveway Wednesday afternoon around 2:00, or a little after, and a neighbor to the Bannister property who saw several vehicles, including a dark-colored vehicle larger than a car, over there Wednesday afternoon. Plus, from the Bannister property we have two different shoe prints and wide tire tread marks. State lab identifies the tire tread as a Goodyear 265/70 R16. Tire dealer in Lynchburg verifies that such a tire size is generally used on full-size SUV's and some pick-up trucks. SO, you can see that we've got a lot more interviewing to do."

Washburn glanced at his legal pad. "Thornton, tell the group about the sport utility vehicles you and your crew have located in that twenty-mile stretch along the river road in Nelson."

A lanky deputy of average height stood. In his hand he held a photocopy of a Polaroid shot of the tire marks found at the Bannister property the previous day, along with a photo of the mold cast. "Our inquiry to DMV for pick-ups and SUV's registered to people with Norwood, Wingina, and Howardsville addresses produced ninety names. So far we've examined thirty-five of the vehicles. No tire matches. We should have the rest of 'em tracked down by tomorrow."

"What about Schuyler, Esmont, and Scottsville addresses?" asked a female rescue worker.

"Right. I was coming to that. Albemarle County deputies are running the check on such vehicles registered to people with those addresses," the deputy answered. "They'll pass on to us the ones with Schuyler addresses that fall across the county line into Nelson. Just as we'll give the Buckingham County sheriff's office the Wingina names and addresses of ones from across the James River."

"Thanks, Thornton. Good work. Now, listen, when *any* of you see pick-up trucks, SUV's, or large vans on the street here in town or at stores and such, get out your photocopy and compare tire treads. Sure doesn't have to be a vehicle found only in the crime scene area," Washburn advised.

He smiled wryly when a collective groan emanated from the group. Then he glanced again at his legal pad. "I see Savidge is not here yet. Bridget, in his place, can you summarize the search efforts to this point?" Washburn asked the female rescue worker who had raised the question about Schuyler, Esmont, and Scottsville.

She stood, consulted a spiral notebook, and said, "I'll try."

Bridget Ashmore, tall and solidly built, had been a volunteer with the rescue squad for twenty years and now served as deputy chief. Her work and dedication had earned her the respect of law enforcement officers in Nelson and surrounding counties.

"At the Dumond property, search dogs lost Mrs. Dumond's scent at the edge of her driveway about twenty feet behind her parked vehicle. Didn't pick up any other fresh scent. Seemed to pick up only faint scent in her garden area, which probably means she had not been there later than a day or two before Wednesday. We found no tire marks, footprints, or other evidence in the half-mile radius of her house. As for the Bannister property, the search teams have found nothing beyond the area where the Michaels vehicle was located and only a partial footprint on a bare spot in the trail between there and the yard. Design in the print was inconclusive."

"Print was heading in which direction?"

"Appeared to be going *toward* the house," Bridget answered.

"And looked like the Polaroid shot I gave you?"

"Possibly. But as I said, inconclusive. Here's a Polaroid we took—not too clear. Maybe forensics can enhance it." She handed the picture to a deputy in front of her, who passed it on to Washburn.

"Great. Thanks, Bridget. Anything else?"

"Well . . . yeah . . . or maybe you know already. Animal Control picked up a dog near the former West Farm entrance about an hour ago. Tired, dirty—"

"The Dumond dog?" Washburn interrupted. "We had notified Animal Control to be on the look-out."

"Maybe. I'm going to the shelter when I leave here. If it generally fits the description that Mrs. Shales gave, I'll be glad to go get her to look—"

"Better still, I'll send Deputy Steele with you. If it looks to you to be Mrs. Dumond's dog, you two can take it on down there to the house for Mrs. Shales to identify," Washburn injected. "And examine it as best you can. Take a couple pictures, too. Okay?"

"Sure. No problem."

"Anyone got anything else?" Washburn asked the group.

Some shook their heads negatively; all looked somewhat downcast. When no one responded, Washburn consulted his legal pad and announced assignments for the day. He left them to discuss details among themselves and to pair-off for the day's work.

He heard his phone ringing before he reached his office door. "Hello. Oh, hello, Blair. How's the ankle?"

"Swollen. But that's not why I'm calling." Her voice oozed excitement.

"Oh?" Washburn felt his heart rate increase.

"I've got a picture for you," she gushed. "Actually, several. Want to send someone here to get them?"

"Hey, hold on! Not so fast. A picture of what?"

"Tire tread!"

"Oh, I have plenty copies of that."

"Not this one, you don't!"

"Well, how about telling me, then," he sparred.

"I took this Polaroid . . . as I said, several . . . from different angles. At Roberta Dumond's place—"

"YOU WHAT! When I expressly told you to stay off that ankle! You've been at your old sleuthing—"

"Whoa, fella! Taking pictures didn't hurt my damn ankle! Besides, I have crutches—"

"Hey . . . hey! Don't get angry. I'm not scolding. I was . . . just concerned," he stuttered a bit, then fell silent for a few seconds. "Where did you find the tire mark?" he asked eventually, trying to sound business-like despite the turmoil of his emotions.

"Off the driveway, about a hundred and fifty feet from the house. Looked like the vehicle was reversed that far, then backed off the pavement a little in order to turn back toward the highway. Good clear tracks in the soft dirt."

"Look like what we . . . what *you* found at the Bannister property?"

"I think so. Pretty sure. Of course, I can't be positive without your picture to compare."

"Well, we'll see. Good work, Blair. I'll drive down—"

"NO!" Blair blurted, too loud. "I mean, you don't need to do that. I can send them in by Richard. You can make molds afterward."

Washburn didn't miss the distress, the tension, in her assertion. "Fine. That'll be fine. Thanks. Take care. Talk to you later," he said bluntly, dismissively, and rang off.

They were both emotionally spent.

"You damn fool," Washburn muttered, "you need to leave it alone!"

Blair simply exhaled audibly.

For the next several hours, Blair tried to stay busy. After cleaning the kitchen, she hobbled to the laundry room, put a load of clothes in the washer, and folded laundry from the dryer. She went from the laundry room upstairs to check on the children's rooms. As usual, Whitley's was reasonably tidy, Meade's generally in a state of chaos. She smiled, loving the individuality of her children. Covers on both beds were straightened in a manner. Good enough, she decided, to hold out for the maid's changing them the next morning.

Downstairs again, she went to her office off the den. It was a small room with plush light gray carpet, bookshelves on one wall, a painting featuring a field full of horses on another wall, a small fireplace across the room from her desk, and a large window overlooking the same farm pond seen from the breakfast room. It was cozy, comfortable, and her personal and private spot in a bustling household. She loved the room, often retreating there to catch up on calls, write letters or notes, and read voraciously. For a few minutes she did nothing but stare out the window at the farm scene. Then she turned to the computer and e-mailed Landis.

Landis had met Peter Mason at the end of their open-house murder investigation the previous October, and they had become a couple soon afterward. They still had separate homes (Peter, the one near Afton that they had sold him), but they spent most of their non-working time together. They seemed to be crazy about each other, but Blair wasn't sure that independent Landis would ever re-marry. At times Blair envied Landis's lifestyle. Most of the time, though, she was grateful for her own. Wasn't she?

"Damn, woman, get off it!" she scolded herself.

When Blair was preparing a snack for lunch, Landis phoned. "Blair, your e-mail . . . I think I'd better fly back now, no matter what you say about not needing me," Landis opened the conversation.

"No, no! Don't do that, Lan. We're making progress with the investigation . . . and there's been no *bad* news. Besides, the cruise ends Tuesday anyway, doesn't it?"

"Yes. But I mean *you*, Blair. You sound so despondent and—"

"LAN, really I'm okay! Well, almost. I mean, hell, under the circumstances—"

"BLAIR, I mean *other* than worrying about Lauren and your friend Roberta!" Landis snapped, overriding Blair's words. "What else is going on . . . bothering you?"

How well my friend knows me, Blair thought. "I'll tell you when you get back Wednesday, okay?"

"Tell me now."

"It's too complicated for the phone. But I'll tell you. I promise. In fact, I really *need* to talk to you."

"Well . . . if you promise. Now, fill me in on progress with the search."

Blair told Landis everything that had happened since e-mailing her the morning before from the office, leaving out only the undercurrent stuff concerning Ned Washburn. No sooner had she hung up, though, than she started to call back and tell Landis to come home *now* after all. She needed her to help with investigating Lauren's disappearance, but, more, she needed . . . "Admit it, Blair, you just need her to smack reality into you," she said aloud.

But she didn't call back. Instead, she looked at her watch and saw that it was only 1:30. "Hell, as they say, it's 5:00 somewhere!" she vented, and went to the frig to pour a glass of wine.

At 5:00 she made a quick call to the sheriff's office to get an updated report but did not ask to speak to Ned Washburn. Instead, she asked for Sheriff Oakley.

"Mrs. Camfield," the sheriff responded, "sorry to say we don't have good news—but no bad news either, as it turns out. One of the search parties gave us quite a scare for awhile, though. Found some bones off old Warminster Road. A vet and a doctor in Amherst say they are animal bones, however—bear or small horse probably—and been exposed a lot longer than two days. Hope to have something better to report soon."

Blair hoped so, too. Fervently.

EIGHT

Natalie Lapplier didn't hate school. Actually she liked it. Most of the time. Today, Friday, however, was another matter entirely. Her sixth grade class project for the day was social dancing conducted by a professional instructor from Richmond. She remembered her teacher saying it was to be a condensed version of ball-room dancing and that it would help young people to develop proper social skills. No way was *she* going to make a fool of herself, getting up in front of her friends and being flung around the floor in the arms of some nerdy old boy who couldn't even hit a baseball as far as she could!

"Natalie, you *know* that's *not* the right outfit for today," her mother said as the girl came into the kitchen. Natalie was wearing jeans and a faded blue sweatshirt. "Here, take this bagel with you and hurry back to your room. Put on that skirt and blouse I bought you last Saturday. And *comb* your hair!"

"Ah, Mom, I can't . . . I just can't go to school today. Please . . . can't I stay home this once?" she pleaded.

"No, honey, you can't. This is important. You *need* to do more girl things—"

"But I *do* girl stuff!" Natalie interrupted. "Plenty. I wear a dress to church. I wash dishes. I vacuum." Natalie paused a second, as if trying to think of something more impressive to list. "I even wear a swimsuit when I go to the Big Hole at the creek with boys."

"Wow, that *is* something!" Anne Lapplier exclaimed, mockingly impressed. Then she moved to Natalie's side, smiled gently, and patted her daughter's shoulder. "That's not the same, Natty. You're eleven now, nearly twelve. Soon you'll be a teen-ager. There're things you need to learn, things you need to experience other than your tomboy interests. This is a start. One day's dancing won't kill you."

"But, Mom—"

"Now *go*! Change clothes quickly, or you'll miss the bus and I'll have to drive you and Eddie to school. By the way, when you pass the bathroom, yell for him to get on to the kitchen. He's been dilly-dallying in there far too long."

Natalie no longer needed to be nudged out of the kitchen. No way could she allow her mother to drive them to school. An idea—a way to escape the horror of dancing up against a stupid boy—was rapidly forming in her head. When her mother turned away and opened the refrigerator, Natalie snatched a plastic grocery bag from a cupboard and exited the room before her mother could see the action. In her bedroom, she took off the jeans, sweatshirt, and sneakers and put them in the plastic bag. Then she removed two textbooks and a notebook from her backpack to make room for the bag of clothes. Scowling and muttering, she slipped into the flouncy skirt, blouse, and slip-on flats, then hastily ran a comb through her curly brown mop.

She re-entered the kitchen to find her nine-year-old brother Eddie sitting at the table with their mother. He was tackling his eggs, bacon, and toast with gusto.

"Now, *that's* my girl!" Anne exclaimed. "So pretty, Natty . . . such a shame you try so hard to hide it."

"Pretty don't mean nothing!" Natty said sulkily. Her bad grammar was a barometer of her foul mood. She dropped her pack beside the back door and flopped into a chair long enough to drink her juice and eat a little cereal.

When the children finished their breakfasts, Anne Lapplier walked with them to the back porch. She kissed each on the cheek.

"Now, scoot," she said jauntily. "And have a great day," she called as they jumped off the last step and started to run down the wooded lane to meet the bus on the county road. Anne stood looking after them until they were out of sight. "Poor Natty," she sympathized aloud, "growing up is surely not going to be easy for you."

At the Lappliers' driveway entrance there was a small enclosed shelter, built by Robert Lapplier for his children to use in bad weather while they waited for the school bus. The structure, painted brown, was about six by eight feet with a window and glass storm door. On the front was a miniature deck with railing. A variety of plantings surrounded it. A cozy real-life doll house.

Almost breathless from the run from home, Natty stepped up on the deck and turned to face Eddie. "Look, promise to keep a secret?"

Eddie loved secrets. "Sure!" he responded enthusiastically.

"Okay. It's like this, see. We're *not* going to school today . . . and you can't tell anybody!"

"But—"

"No but's. You promised."

"All's I was gonna say was '*why*'," he defended.

"I'm just *not* going to do that dern old dance thing at school, that's all! I've got my jeans and stuff in here," she said, patting her backpack. "I'm gonna change into 'em while you stand guard out here. Then we're going fishing!" she finished.

"Hot dog!" Eddie exclaimed. He never needed much persuasion to follow his big sister into mischief. After all, if they got into trouble, she always took the blame. No risk to him. Eddie was an energetic boy, but a sense of responsibility was not high on his list of characteristics.

Natty changed clothes quickly, leaving the outfit she removed with their backpacks under a bench at the rear of the building. She knew there was not much chance of her mother going inside before she and Eddie would return at approximately the time of the school bus's afternoon run, and her father had already gone to work. Outside again, she encountered Eddie stridently confronting her, hands on his skinny hips.

"What are we supposed to do for fishing poles and stuff?" he demanded, thinking he had caught a slip in her planning.

"Get 'em from the garage, silly."

"How? Mom will see us for sure."

"No, she won't. We'll go 'round through the woods to the back. I already unlocked the rear window. You're gonna crawl in and get our rods and Dad's tackle box. No problem."

"How come *I* have to crawl in?"

"Because you're smaller, squirt. And besides you can do it better than I can," she added to spike his ego and hush his objections. "Now, come on, let's move. We don't want to be standing here when the bus comes 'round the curve."

They ducked around the shelter and scurried headlong uphill, skirting the driveway by a couple hundred feet as they made their way back to the open area where the house, garage, and outbuildings were located. They circled the open area, remaining obscured in the woods until they approached the rear of the garage. As they left the woods, they bent forward so much that they were practically walking on all-fours. They covered the hundred feet of open area, looking like primates sneaking up on prey.

Flattened tight against the back wall of the garage, Natty shushed Eddie. "Be quiet a minute," she whispered. "Listen for anybody coming—in case they saw us." After a few minutes of silence, punctuated only by their loud breathing, she slipped to the corner and peeped around to survey the rear of the house. No one was in sight, and the only sound carried to her ears was the faint voice of a talk-show host. Her mother had turned on the radio they kept on a window ledge in the kitchen and was listening while she did household chores.

"Coast is clear," Natty hissed. "Here, lemme give you a hoist," she said, closing in behind him. "Grab the window ledge. Say when you're ready."

Natty cupped her hands and bent over. Eddie jumped off the ground about a foot and grasped the window ledge above. "Ready," he squeaked.

Natty clasped her cupped hands beneath Eddie's sneakered feet and, grunting big time, gave a powerful heave-ho. Eddie's body shot through the window and thudded to the floor inside. But not before Natty heard a tearing sound and Eddie's yelping "Ow-oh!"

"What happened?" she hissed.

"Caught my tail on a nail!" he hissed back.

"Hurry up. Get the stuff and get out!"

Natty slipped back to the corner and sneaked another glance at the house. Nothing stirred. She returned to the window just as Eddie pushed two fishing rods through. She lowered them to the ground. He pushed the tackle box to the ledge. She lunged upward to reach it and set it on the ground beside the rods. "Now, come on!" she commanded.

"I can't get up to the window," he returned.

"Then find something to stand on, stu—." Natty cut herself off before finishing *stupid.* This was no time to antagonize her little brother.

She heard a tinny, rattling sound, followed by a sort of thump. Suddenly sunlight caught on Eddie's shiny blond hair. Next she saw his thin arms and scrawny chest pull over the ledge, just as she heard a metal object fall and roll.

"What the heck was that?" Natty snapped, scared the noise had reached the house.

Face, shoulders, and arms dangling outside the window, Eddie managed only to gasp, "Oil can. Help me down quick, Natty!"

Natty caught him under the shoulders, got him turned onto his back, and slid him down the white-painted wall—leaving a long red smear in his wake.

"What's that?" she asked, stepping closer to the wall for a look-see when Eddie was back on his feet. "Blood!" she screeched, turning pale.

"Nail tore my britches . . . cut my ass . . . and it hurts, too," Eddie complained, turning his backside for her to see the proof. There was a six-inch tear in his jeans beside the right hip pocket. She could see his blood-stained white briefs beneath.

"Oh, gosh . . . oh, shoot . . . Well, come on, let's get out of sight in the woods. Then I'll see if Dad has a first-aid kit in that tackle box."

They moved back across the open area to the woods, again bending double as they scurried. Once within tree cover, they turned and looked back. No one was in sight and no human voice could be heard. Natty opened the tackle box and removed a bottle.

"What's that?" Eddie asked.

"Drop your jeans and drawers," Natty commanded, ignoring his question.

"No! . . . I ain't taking my britches off! Unk-uh . . . No way!" Eddie spat, backing away several steps.

"I didn't say take 'em off. Just turn around and lower 'em a little so's I can see the cut better." When he hesitated still, she commanded between gritted teeth, "*Do it now*!"

Mumbling incoherently, Eddie reluctantly did as she had directed. A three-inch ragged-edge cut stretched down his right buttock. Bleeding had stopped. Her cursory examination satisfied Natty that the cut was not deep, but she knew from her parents' warnings in the past that a wound caused by a rusted nail could be dangerous. She opened the bottle of iodine and sloshed the liquid on the cut—top to bottom.

"Ow-oh! Ow-oh!" Eddie howled at the top of his lungs when the medicine hit the raw wound.

Natty slammed into his backside, sending him sprawling face-down in thick pine needles.

"Shut up!" she hissed, grabbing his arm and jerking him to his feet. "Don't be such a baby. You want the whole community to hear you?"

Eddie yanked his arm free, sputtering away the pine needles plastered to his lips. His face was red, and his eyes shot daggers at his sister. As he snatched up his jeans, he blurted, "I don't care . . . I don't even want to go with you no more!"

Natty knew it was time to employ diplomacy. "Ah, Eddie, I'm sorry. Just trying to help . . . to make you feel better so's you can catch the biggest ole fish in the river. You want to do that, don't you?"

The trick worked—as always—for the gullible Eddie. "Well . . . I reckon," he conceded. "But what we gonna do for bait?" he asked peevishly.

"Minnows. We'll wade Slaytor Creek."

"How we gonna catch 'em, Natty? You thought of that?" he challenged, determined to hold onto his sulkiness as long as possible to spite Natty.

"Yep. Tommy left his dad's net and bucket down by the bridge. Pick up the poles. Let's get going."

Eddie didn't protest further. But his enthusiasm for the adventure had waned—what with the pain in his butt and the injury to his dignity!

They reached the creek without discovery. A gully overgrown with wild privet hid their passage downhill through the field area of a pasture, and a strip of trees between the field and the creek provided them cover over the flat area visible from the county road. Only at the creek bank when they stopped to catch their breath did they relax. So far, so good. Looked now like they would have a truly free day, Natty thought. She exhaled loudly and smiled. A free day the more exhilerating because it was her creation—and a hateful school assignment dodged in the bargain! She knelt to to take off her sneakers and socks.

"Eddie, I'll go get the bucket and net. You can put the hooks and sinkers on the lines, okay?" she said, as she rolled her jeans up to her knees.

"Ar-ite," he grunted, proceeding to sit on a boulder before opening the tackle box.

Natty turned left downstream, hopping on flat stones in the creek when she reached them and wading in clear shallow water when no stones were available. The creek bottom was mostly covered with tiny pebbles, which tickled her bare soles. In patches the bottom was fine tan-colored sand, cushioning her feet as if they were stepping on wool flannel. The water was still comfortably warm even though it was the second week in October. She hummed her school song as she skipped the hundred feet or so to the county-road bridge.

Halfway on the return upstream to where she had left Eddie, Natty was startled to hear raspy coughing. "Oh, rats," she muttered. "Now what?" She splashed through water on the run, not looking for stepping-stones now. Rounding a bend in the creek, she stopped short. Eddie stood on the bank, two feet higher than water level. He was bent forward at the waist, vomiting the contents of his breakfast into the stream.

"Yuk!" Natty scoffed, revolted. "What happened?" she hollered.

Eddie pointed backward toward the boulder where he had sat to ready the fishing gear. His retching prevented his talking. Natty moved closer to the boulder. Lying on the black soil at the base of the boulder was a still-burning cigar.

"Geez, Eddie, are you okay?" she asked, feigning sympathy.

Straightening a little and turning toward his sister, he gasped, "I dunno. Think I'm gonna die!"

"Gee gads, Ed, where did you get that thing? What were you thinking?" Natty was working hard to clean up her language, substituting expressions such as "gee gads" for the salty words which had gotten her sent to the principal's office twice when classmates had reported her for "cussing like a sailor" on the playground. Not only did she not want to get reported again, she now thought that broadening her vocabulary would be a sign to others that she was "growing up".

"Shelf . . . in the . . . garage," Eddie managed to string out, as he shuffled back to the boulder.

Their father didn't smoke, but a couple of his friends did. And their cousin Aubrey smoked, too, Natty remembered. One of them must have left the cigar, she figured. Pulling off a couple paper towels from the half-roll in the tackle box, Natty stepped to the creek and dipped them. Then she returned to the boulder and wiped Eddie's face, patting the area between his shoulder blades simultaneously. Before he could react, she took a stick of Juicy Fruit from a pack in her back pocket and unwrapped it.

"Look here," she commanded. He faced upward. "Open," she directed, and shoved the gum between his lips. He opened his mouth and sucked in the gum before it could drop. "Feel better now, don'tcha?"

"Some . . . I reckon," Eddie muttered, shifting the wad of gum to the other cheek. "But mebbe I oughta go on home—"

"NO!" Natty interrupted, her emphatic tone echoing off the rock bluff across the creek. "Get your snivelling butt up and come on!"

Eddie stood. And staggered a little when he reached down for the fishing rods.

"Leave the da . . . the stupid poles, Eddie, for go . . . heaven's sake!" Natty snapped. "We're wading upstream for minnows first. We'll pick up that stuff coming back. Now, get your shoes off and come on! Bring the bucket."

Natty picked up the net, waded into the creek, and started pulling the net through the water. From fifty or sixty feet upstream, she heard Eddie jump off the bank behind her, probably splashing himself from top to bottom. Eddie's mishaps were beginning to make her a little weary already—and the adventure had barely started. But what alternative had she had, she reminded herself—and sped up her efforts.

Forty-five minutes later they returned to their equipment stash. A good-size knot of minnows thrashed in the bucket, now half filled with water and covered with the rimmed net. Natty elected to carry the bucket. With Eddie's luck, she figured he would likely spill all their catch before they got to the river. She also volunteered to carry the rods in her other hand, leaving only the tackle box for Eddie to handle. They carried their shoes hanging from their necks, tied together by the laces. Just before reaching the bridge, they waded the creek, stopped to put on socks and shoes, then set off uphill in the woods paralleling the north side of the road. At the top of the hill they stepped to the woods' edge and looked along the road in both directions. Nothing in sight.

"All right, Eddie, crouch and stay close behind me. I'm gonna dash across the road and then keep on running until we're past the schoolhouse. Ready?"

Eddie nodded. They hit the road at full tilt—and didn't stop until they were past the building and well obscured from the road. They stopped briefly to rest. Natty sat down on a low bank along the farm road leading to an old abandoned farmhouse. She looked back at the two-room schoolhouse where her grandmother had attended early grades. Closed as a school nearly sixty years earlier and abandoned for the past thirty-five years, the structure was now dilapidated and vine-covered. Spooky looking. Shuddering slightly, Natty was glad it was daytime. She had heard lots of scary stories about the place—like peculiar noises inside late at night.

"Come on," she said to Eddie, getting up quickly and retrieving the bucket and poles. They set off along the edge of a huge hay field. Natty didn't think the absentee owner would mind.

They didn't stop again until they reached the spot along the railroad tracks where a village once existed. Not a single structure remained. No one to see them. They skipped the hundred yards to the long-abandoned boat landing, baited their hooks, and sat down to wait for a bite.

Two hours later they had caught only one eel and one very small catfish, both of which they released back into the river. Growing bored eventually, they sang for awhile—the same three songs repeatedly. When he tired of the singing, Eddie propped his rod against a fallen willow tree and turned to building a sand castle.

"I'm hungry," Eddie blurted at one o'clock, according to Natty's old wristwatch.

"Me, too," Natty echoed. She pulled a plastic zip-lock bag from the tackle box. A cigarette lighter, snagged by the bag, dropped to the sand beside her. Idly she picked it up and put it in her pocket before opening the bag and removing two Snickers bars.

"Hey, where'd they come from?" Eddie squealed with delight.

"I had 'em in my backpack, put 'em in my sweatshirt pouch, then stashed 'em in the tackle box when I got out the iodine."

"Cool! Wonder I didn't see 'em. Here, gimme one."

They ate the candy in silence. When Natty finished her bar, she snatched some broomsage from a cluster behind her and rolled the straw up in the Snickers wrapper.

"Hey, Eddie, look! Let *me* show you how to smoke," she bragged. She put the ready-roll in her mouth, pulled the lighter from her pocket and fired away. The dry broomstraw flared like a torch. Natty spat out the burning mess as fast as she could—but not before it singed a lock of hair on her forehead and burned one finger.

"Hells bells!" Natty exclaimed as she jumped up to stomp out the flaming residue. Eddie rolled on the ground, guffawing so hard that tears began to stream down his cheeks.

"Ha . . . Ha . . . Joke's on you!" he taunted several times, stopping only when she dramatically stomped toward him with fist raised.

When their moods cooled, they re-baited their hooks and tried fishing for most of another hour. Nothing even nibbled. A little before two o'clock they called quits to the "adventure", packed up, and headed home.

Reaching the old schoolhouse, they cut behind it and slipped downhill to the creek on the south side of the county road. At the creek Natty stopped to release the remaining living minnows into the water. Eddie turned upstream toward the bridge, carrying the tackle box.

"Ooh-o . . . ooh-o . . . ooh-o . . . !" Eddie's blood-curdling screams reached Natty's ears just as she saw him running full-steam back toward her, jumping low growth and flailing bushes aside with wide-spread arms. The front of his faded jeans showed that he had had an accident. He was steamy wet from crotch to ankles!

"What the he . . . heck now? STOP it, Eddie! SHUT UP!" she commanded between clenched teeth when his screaming continued.

"Nat . . . at . . . e . . . Oh, Oh!" Eddie squeaked as he dropped to the ground in front of her, wild-eyed and breathless.

"What's wrong with you anyway? You look like you saw a ghost." Despite her dismissive question, Natty was beginning to sense something bad. Even Eddie was not prone to hysterics.

"Did a bee sting you? See a snake—"

"No-o-o! A bo . . . a bod . . . y. It . . . ah . . ." he gasped, hiccups taking over his ability to speak. He appeared to strangle on his saliva, then began to heave.

"Eddie! Get a grip! What do you mean . . . a body?"

"Up there . . . close to the bridge . . . laying on the bank," he sputtered.

"For crap's sake! I'll go look . . . but if you're playing a trick . . . I'll . . ." she trailed off without stating a threat, already walking toward the bridge.

Natty came upon the body before she reached the area that Eddie had seemed to describe.

"Oh shit!" she muttered, momentarily clamping hands over her eyes. It certainly never occurred to her to clean up her language in such circumstances.

She removed her hands slowly. It was no illusion. A body *was* lying on the bank in knee-high wild ferns, perhaps seventy feet from the bridge and no more than fifty feet from a ford in the creek where some people washed their cars. She stepped closer. The body was lying on its stomach, the head turned toward the creek. From the back Natty noted tousled wavy hair, a dark long-sleeved top, gray slacks, and black one-inch slippers on the stockinged feet. It was a woman.

"Don't panic," she told herself. "Think. What to do? Maybe she's just drunk or sleeping or something."

Natty picked up a dead tree branch. She moved a little closer and stretched the stick out to touch the woman's back. Nervousness caused her to push a bit harder than she had intended. The woman's shoulder moved slightly forward and then relaxed back into place.

Startled by the movement, Natty took a step backward. Her heel caught on a tree root and she splattered to the ground. She sat up quickly. "Ma'am? Ma'am, are you okay?"

There was no answer. Natty got up and approached the area of the woman's feet. She reached down and touched fingers to one ankle. It was cold and hard. And suddenly an awful odor stung her nostrils. She stumbled away, gasping. She grabbed at the trunk of an oak tree, leaned over, and lost the remnants of her candy bar and breakfast. Never had she felt anything like the woman's ankle or smelled such an odor, but instinctively she knew from the sensations that the woman was indeed dead.

After a few minutes Natty straightened. She wiped her face on the sleeve of her sweatshirt, brushed at the seat of her jeans, and walked back to Eddie. Consciously she put on a blank expression for his benefit, knowing she had to comfort him . . . protect him . . . as she *always* did—if only in her backassward fashion. What a day she had put him through just to help cover up her own deceit! Looked like she would owe him for quite awhile.

Natty glanced at her watch. They needed to hurry.

"Eddie, where's the tackle box?"

"I . . . don't . . . I dropped it."

"Okay, come on. We'll pick it up on the way to return the bucket and net to the bridge."

"I ain't going back that way! And you can't make me neither," he protested petulantly.

"Just forget it, then! Cross the creek here and go on to the bus stop. Take the damn rods with you. And hurry! But wait for me there. You hear me, Eddie?" she demanded when he didn't acknowledge her instructions.

"Yeah, I heard ya," he grumbled.

"Then get going!"

Natty marched off toward the bridge. She was thinking that maybe she wouldn't owe Eddie a dern thing after all. He could be such a little snot! But the need to concentrate on how to handle her present predicament quickly evaporated her anger. What a miserable day it had turned out to be! All she had wanted was to avoid a class assignment. Now she faced confrontations with not only her parents, the school principal, and her teacher—but also the *police*!

"Oh God!" she whispered.

Then with lowered head and hunched shoulders she marched on to face the music.

NINE

"Where's Eddie, Natty?" Anne Lapplier asked as she prepared dinner. "I haven't seen him since he came home from school."

"In his room. I don't think he wants dinner. Said he doesn't feel very good."

"Really? Come to think of it, he didn't seem himself. I'd better go check," Anne said and hastily left the kitchen.

Robert Lapplier looked up from the chopping block, where he was preparing their salads. "Nat, how was school today?" he asked.

"Okay, I think."

"The dance lesson go all right?"

"I guess so."

Noncommittal answers weren't lies, were they? Natty prided herself on not lying; she just didn't always tell the whole truth.

"Eddie says his stomach hurts," Anne announced, walking back into the kitchen. "Natty, here's a spoon. Get the Pepto from the hall bathroom, will you, and make him take a couple spoonfuls?"

"Sure."

"Whew, what a relief!" Natty said under her breath as she sidled out of the kitchen and then ran down the hall.

Eddie had left it up to her to report the day's events. And so far she had chickened out.

"You tell yet?" Eddie asked the second she walked into his room. He was in bed, under covers, still dressed.

"No. Did you say anything to Mom?"

"NO-O! I ain't saying *nothing*! To *nobody*. It was your idea to skip. Now *you* gotta tell 'em!"

"I will . . . I *will*! I said I would, didn't I? I just have to get it straight in my head first. Here, drink this stuff."

"I don't wanna."

"Drink it anyway. Might settle your stomach."

Eddie swallowed the medicine that Natty spoonfed him. She took a slug herself, straight from the bottle.

"Now, get undressed and wash up. I'll bring you a snack later," she promised, then left his room.

Natty didn't demonstrate her usual appetite at dinner either. She choked down a couple bites of meat and veggies, then just pushed the remaining food around on her plate. And she didn't chatter away as usual. Her mom and dad didn't notice right away; they were occupied talking to each other about the events of their day.

"Why so quiet, Nat?" her dad finally asked. Noticing the food left on her plate, he added, "You sick, too?"

"No. Just tired."

"All that dancing wore you down, huh?"

"I'm sure she's had a rough day," her mom followed up. "You're excused, Natty. Go rest awhile. You can have a snack later if you want."

"Thanks."

Natty hurried to her room and undressed for the fifth time in one day. After a lengthy bot bath, she put on pajamas and crawled into bed. "Maybe I do need a little rest . . . to make confessing easier," she murmurred as her head sank into the soft pillow. She was out like a light.

Blood-curdling screams from Eddie's room jolted Natty awake. She dashed into the hall. So had her mom and dad rushed out of their bedroom. They all stopped short when they met. No one spoke. The parents stared at their daughter for a fixed moment. Anne Lapplier reacted first. She frowned, denoting both perplexion and a dawning perception. Her children were hiding something she was almost sure. But what?

Robert Lapplier opened Eddie's door. The boy lay sprawled on his bed, face down and sobbing. Both parents rushed to him. Natty hung back at the doorway. Robert turned his son over and lifted him into a sitting position, and Anne, sitting on the bedside opposite, gently pushed Eddie's hair back from his forehead. She wiped his face with a tissue, and noted that he was not feverish.

"What is it, son?" Robert asked, keeping an arm around the boy's shoulders.

Eddie sobbed convulsively.

"Honey . . . honey, it's all right. We're right here," Anne cooed, crawling onto the bed to embrace her son. "Did you have a nightmare?"

Eddie nodded affirmatively.

"Can you tell us about it?" Robert pursued.

Eddie lifted his head slightly and glanced at Natty. Both parents turned eyes toward the doorway. It was empty. Robert lunged off the bed and rushed to the hall. He looked into Natty's room. No Natty. He caught up with her in the kitchen. She stood behind a chair at the table, her back to him.

"Natalie!" he barked. She winced. Her dad never called her by her given name unless he meant serious business.

"Natalie," he said again, but more gently. "Turn around." When she faced him, with head down, he continued, "Come here. Let's go back to Eddie's room."

Natty preceeded her dad down the hallway. Just inside Eddie's room, he put his arm around her and guided her to the foot of Eddie's bed.

"Now, Eddie, here she is. What were you going to say to her?" Robert asked, still holding Natty.

"Nothin'. I wadn't gonna say nothin', Natty," Eddie protested, bottom lip protruding.

"All right, then, Natty, do you have something to tell us?"

Silence.

Robert let the silence run a full minute. He exchanged glances with his wife, and winked to convey that he had a strategy.

"Okay," he began, breaking what Natty thought an interminable silence, "it's now six-thirty in the morning. And Saturday. So we'll all stay right here, just like this, until one of you decides to 'fess up. No matter how long it takes. Your mother and I know now that something happened yesterday, something that upset Eddie—scared him silly apparently—and that made you, Natty, become quiet as a mouse. Go take a seat at Eddie's desk. Your mother and I will sit over here by the window. Let us know when you're ready to talk. Either one of you."

Anne joined her husband on the cobbler's bench. They closed their eyes and leaned back. Natty picked at her fingernails, then chewed off several. Eddie pulled the sheet over his face. A cricket hidden somewhere in a corner or in the hall began a loud chirping. Ten, twenty, thirty minutes passed. Still no one spoke.

Forty-five minutes into the test of wills, restless Eddie couldn't stand the suspense any longer. He threw off the sheet.

"Natty," he implored, "you gotta tell. I can't stand this no longer!"

Natty levelled a look at her brother. The lack of defiance in her expression, the lack of anger, surprised him. He had fully expected to get a real tongue-lashing from her.

"Dad, Mom . . . I'm ready to talk," she said simply, sounding calmly resigned—and somehow very grown-up.

A half-hour later Robert Lapplier phoned the sheriff's office. Before investigators arrived, he outlined the children's punishment for their day of "misadventure". It was to include no after-school activities for two weeks, notes written by each of them to their teachers, no Halloween party for either—and *dance* lessons for Natty.

To boot, she would have to lead her father and the deputies to the body.

Playing hookey for one day had certainly cost her dearly. "Sometimes life just sucks, is all," she concluded in thought, somehow sensing that a big phase of childhood had ended for her. For good.

TEN

Ned Washburn and Deputy Taskell arrived at the Lapplier residence at 8:15. Natty and her father met them in the driveway and climbed into the back seat of the cruiser to direct the officers to the ford at Slaytor Creek.

"Did you disturb the body, young lady? Natty, is it?" Washburn asked as he crossed the bridge and made a U-turn down to the ford on the west side of the creek.

"What do you mean?" Natty asked hautily, challenged.

"Move it, touch it."

"Oh no, sir. I didn't move her. I only put a finger on one ankle. To see if she was asleep or something." Natty didn't mention poking the woman's back with a stick. She didn't see any need for that; they might think she had been scared.

"Fine. Then let's go take a look," Washburn said, opening his door and getting out. "Lead the way, young lady," he directed Natty when they were all outside.

Natty scowled fiercely upon hearing the second reference to her as "young lady". She opened her mouth to reprimand Washburn, but Robert Lapplier saw her intention in time to move quickly to his daughter's side and grab her elbow. She got the silent message. All four walked downslope together to the water's edge, then turned south along the creek bank. Natty stopped ten feet from the body and pointed. Washburn and Taskell leaned forward to examine the ground in the immediate area around the body before approaching it.

"Here's a partial footprint, Captain. Looks kinda small," Deputy Taskell announced.

Washburn knelt to check it. A shallow imprint of a shoe showed in a small bare spot left by a dislodged rock. A rock that Natty had kicked loose when she fell the afternoon before.

"Natty, lift your right foot . . . let me see your shoe sole," Washburn directed.

Natty crossed her right leg over her left knee and rested a hand on her father's arm for balance. "Those the same sneakers you had on yesterday when you were here?" he asked.

"Yeah."

"Thanks. You can put your foot down now. This print belongs to the girl," he told Deputy Taskell in a tone loud enough for Natty and her father to hear, too. "Keep looking. For any kind of sign."

Washburn himself moved closer to the body. He removed a camera from a shoulder carry-all and proceeded to take numerous pictures from various angles. Just as he finished, an unmarked black van drove up behind the police cruiser. It was the doctor who served as county coroner. Washburn had called him and given directions to the scene as soon as he had reached the Lapplier residence.

Deputy Taskell walked back closer to the bridge and waved the doctor down to their location. He approached, carrying a body bag. No one said anything during the next few minutes while the doctor-coroner performed a peripheral examination, hands gloved.

"Skull crushed. Don't see other obvious wounds," he said as he stood from his squatting position.

"How long's she been dead, doc?" Washburn asked.

"More'n forty-eight hours, maybe as long as seventy-two. Can't be exact before autopsy, maybe not then—but closer." Doctor Raymond was a word minimalist, to be sure. Never unfriendly, just always to the point. "Recognize her?"

"I don't. Not in such condition. But she might be this person," Washburn said, pulling a photo from his inside jacket pocket.

The doctor glanced at the photo. "Don't know," he said. "You finished with her?"

"Yes. For now."

Dr. Raymond unfolded the body bag and laid it on the ground. "Gimme a hand bagging and loading," he commanded.

"Sure. But just a minute. Mr. Lapplier, take Natty back to my car, will you?"

"Of course," Lapplier responded. "Come on, Nat."

"Orie," Washburn said, nodding toward the doctor and the body, "give me a hand."

Washburn and the deputy slipped on plastic gloves and lifted the body while the doctor slid the bag under her.

"WAIT!" Washburn shouted just before the doctor finished zipping the bag.

"What?" Dr. Raymond asked, plainly startled—and puzzled.

"On her blouse. Zip back to her chest."

Dr. Raymond unzipped the bag to waist level. "What'd you see?"

"A hair . . . on her shoulder. Not her color," Washburn answered. He picked up the strand of hair and held it gingerly between thumb and forefinger. "Orie, reach one of the evidence bags in my jacket pocket and open it for me, will you? Right side pocket."

Once in the baggy, the hair could be observed without risk of contamination. "Funny color," Deputy Taskell commented.

"Yeah. I'd say probably not natural. More'n likely a dye job," Washburn speculated.

"Call it red?" Dr. Raymond queried.

"Certainly a variation of red, I'd say," Washburn qualified.

"And Jane Doe's hair is brown, with a few grays," Deputy Taskell said, pointing out the obvious.

"Let's get her loaded," the doctor said, re-zipping the body bag.

"Orie, go get the van. Back it down to the ford. I think Doc and I can tote her that far without your help."

At the ford they lowered the bag to the ground and waited for the van. Washburn used the intervening couple minutes to examine the gravelly soil. He saw something immediately. In a slightly moist spot in loam about six feet from the water's edge was the clear imprint of a wide tire tread. He knelt and photographed it, then stood and photographed it in the context of the bridge and ford environment. Afterward, he stepped over the imprint and raised his arms to signal Deputy Taskell to stop the van before backing over the imprint.

The two officers lifted the body bag into the rear section of the van.

"Doc, I'll call a couple family members of the two missing women. You taking her to the funeral home first?"

"Yep. Long enough for identification. Then she's on to Richmond for autopsy."

"Thanks. I'll be right along—as soon as I take Lapplier and his daughter home. Meanwhile, I'll phone Deputy Hank Parker to come help Taskell make a cast of the tire track and tape off the scene, etc."

On the way back to their home, Washburn questioned the father and child about the lapse of time from discovery of the body to time of reporting it. Natty rode in the back seat, her dad up front with the officer.

"So what were you thinking, Natty?" Washburn asked, catching her eye in the rear view mirror. "If your parents hadn't suspected you were hiding something and gotten you to confess, what did you expect to happen?"

"That somebody else would find her."

"Why'd you think that?"

"Because her family would know she was missing . . . and people would be out looking for her."

"But suppose no one found her? What then?"

"I . . . I don't know . . . I . . . ," Natty broke off.

"Officer, she's just a child!" Robert Lapplier cautioned, defending his daughter.

"I know she is, sir. I just want to impress upon her the importance of being truthful—"

"I didn't lie!" Natty interrupted to defend herself hotly. "I *don't* lie. I . . . just don't tell everything sometimes. I didn't tell about the woman because we were cutting school. I'm *sorry*! But YOU know about her now. And *I* sure don't plan on getting involved in a mess like this anymore!" she finished emphatically.

"Good! That's *very* good. And you've been very helpful, Natty. I want to thank you for that."

"You're welcome," Natty returned, calm now and sounding very adult. "Will I have to go to court?"

"For what?"

"To testify, of course. That's what happens on TV."

"Oh. I see. Well, probably not in this case. Naturally, you'd have to testify if you had *seen* a crime occurring—or could *identify* someone involved in a crime."

"Well, that's okay then. But let me know if you need me to help with anything else," Natty offered.

Washburn smiled. And winked at the father.

En route to Lovingston, Washburn phoned Della Dumond Shales and Blair Camfield, reported the discovery of a body, and asked them to meet him at the funeral home.

The doctor greeted Washburn at the funeral home's side door. "We put her on a guerney in there," Dr. Raymond explained, gesturing over his shoulder toward an ante-room to the embalming and body prep room. "Thought it better than out in the van or hearse for family members to see the body."

"Good thinking. Thanks, Doc."

"Cleaned her up a bit, too. Just cosmetically."

The words were barely spoken when their attention was directed to a speeding car braking to a skidding stop on the wrong side of Front Street.

"What the—" the doctor began.

"Mrs. Camfield, I expect," Washburn cut in, already in a running-walk toward the building's entrance.

Blair had reached the front porch and was pulling at the locked door when Washburn rounded the corner.

"Blair!" he yelled. She did a three-quarter turn, trying to locate the caller, before her gaze fell on Washburn standing in the side driveway.

"Oh, Ned! Where—" she began, then turned abruptly and bounded down the porch steps. She lurched across the spate of grass and stopped at his side. Only then did she lift her left foot, wincing as pain finally registered.

"You okay?" he asked urgently, grasping her arm to steady her.

"Yes . . . no. So upset . . . nervous. Just forgot about my ankle. It's not so bad . . . I'm okay. Really."

"This way, then," he responded gently, guiding her up the driveway.

"Is it Lauren, do you think?"

"I don't think so . . . but . . . I mean, it may have been as much as two and a half days—"

"I know. Don't say any more. Will I be shocked?"

"Some, I expect. But . . . considering, she's not in bad shape."

They had reached the doctor, who still stood beside his van at the side door.

"Blair, this is Doctor Raymond. Doc, this is Blair Cam—"

"Yes, I know her. How are you, Mrs. Camfield?"

"I'm . . . well, I'm . . ."

"Never mind. I understand. Come this way," he directed, holding open the door.

Blair preceeded him inside, Washburn following. The funeral director, Garry Weldon, a sandy-haired man in his mid-forties, approached them immediately. Washburn introduced Blair.

"I know Mrs. Camfield already," Weldon said. "We see each other sometimes at lunch—Vito's or the Cafe." He took her left hand and pulled it through the crook of his right arm. She smiled at Washburn and dropped her other hand from his arm. He and the doctor followed her and the director into the room and to the guerney on the far side.

When the funeral director released her hand and turned to the sheet covering the dead woman's body, Washburn put his arm around Blair's shoulders. "You ready?" he asked her, a little above a whisper.

"Yes," she responded more strongly than she felt.

Washburn nodded to the director, who then gently pulled the sheet back to the woman's waist. She was still fully clothed.

Blair gasped. Washburn tightened his grip on her upper arm. "It's . . . Roberta Dumond," she announced huskily. Pent-up tears broke loose and streaked her cheeks.

"You sure?" Washburn asked.

"Yes. Absolutely. But Della will confirm my identification for you . . . make it official."

"Of course," the doctor and Washburn said simultaneously.

"Poor Bert," Blair went on, undeterred by their comment, "such a gentle, kind, caring soul. Never hurt anyone. Who would do this to her?"

"We'll find whoever it is!" Washburn promised, his voice hoarse. Blair's tears had torn at his hardened official heartstrings.

"Mrs. Camfield, can I get you a glass of water? Or anything?" the funeral director asked.

"Thank you, no."

"Come on, I'll walk you to your car," Washburn invited.

"No. I'll wait outside for Bert's daughter," Blair countered.

"You needn't do that," the funeral director put in quickly. "You can wait in my office. It's just through there," he added, pointing to a door on the side of the room. "Come with me."

Della Dumond Shales arrived a few minutes after 10:00, positively identified her mother, and stayed on to discuss post-autopsy funeral arrangements with the funeral director. After chatting briefly with Della and expressing her desire to assist with a memorial service, Blair limped to her car. Washburn was waiting for her.

"Blair," he announced, "the dog found down Route 626 *is* Roberta Dumond's missing dog. Ironically, in another mile or so he would have found his mistress."

Blair's eyes filled with tears. "Ned, do you think Lauren, too—"

"NO! And don't you think it! Lauren wasn't at the Bannister property, no one has reported seeing her since Wednesday, and no other body has been found. I think someone may be holding her somewhere. And we're gonna get a good lead from somebody soon! In fact, deputies have lined up seven interviews for me—with people they've talked to along the James. I'm going straight there in a few minutes. Also want to talk to the head of a hunt club down there—"

"*Seven* interviews! The deputies have talked with them already and think there's reason for you to pursue further? Who are they?"

"Let's see," Washburn mused, reaching into his inside jacket pocket for his small notebook. He thumbed over a number of pages before stopping. "Here we are. There's a semi-hermit writer who lives in a trailer behind the house on the Laynesville Estate; two fishermen camping at Midway Mills Game Preserve; a farmer-logger and his wife; a traveler at the Howardsville convenience store; and a minister of some persuasion or other. Deputies couldn't get the straight of it. And while I'm down there I want to talk to those two men at the store again."

"A minister? Who?"

"Don't think they put down a name for him. Wait a minute . . . maybe this is meant to be it. Looks like Deputy Brown wrote Neverdoo—or something strange like that."

"Close, if it's Netherdon. He's been kicked out of a couple churches. Been trying to get into mine."

"Really? So . . . Roberta Dumond's church, huh?"

"Yes."

"Huumm . . . interesting. Want to go with me?" Washburn asked, somewhat timidly.

"Yes . . . very much. But I think it best that I not. I . . ."

"No need to explain. I'll let you know any developments, okay? Stay off that foot as much as you can, hear?"

"Sure. And, Ned . . . thanks."

"For what?" he asked, his eyes teasing.

"For your . . . you . . . for everything. Good-bye, Ned," Blair finished abruptly and turned to her car door, afraid to look at him any longer.

Washburn reached around her and opened the door. She hesitated a moment, then slid onto the seat, looking straight ahead over the steering wheel. He closed the door softly, touched fingers to the glass, then turned his back and walked away quickly to the funeral home driveway. Blair started her car, glanced at the side mirror, then drove away from the curb without looking back in Washburn's direction.

Washburn's interviews with the two fishermen, the traveler, and the store proprietor along with his side-kick Bim were routine, unproductive, and almost non-time consuming. All had alibis for the previous Wednesday and could provide no tips leading to a suspect. Interviews with the rather eccentric "writer", the farmer and wife, and the minister were a bit more complicated.

The writer had no vehicle of any kind, but to account for his whereabouts on Wednesday he put Washburn through a long rigamorole of decoding journal scribblings that recorded the dates and hours he had spent writing during the past month. Washburn felt lucky to get away after more than two hours. The writer, he felt, would himself be lucky indeed to get published in the next two decades!

A visit to the farmer, and sometime-logger, and his homemaker wife followed. Randy Millard was a muscular specimen with a transparent down-country friendly and frank nature. His open countenance stated to the world, "What you see is what you get; take it or leave it". His wife, Shirley, by contrast, was tightlipped and unhappy looking. Her mouth turned downward and there were no laugh lines beside her eyes. Without her sour expression, unfriendly attitude, and head turban, however, she could have been a fairly attractive woman, Washburn conceded mentally.

After introducing himself on the porch and briefly stating the purpose of his visit, Washburn addressed Randy Millard first, while glancing at Shirley from time to time.

"Mr. Millard, do you know anyone down this way who drives a dark-colored van or—"

"Hell, man, nearly every family's got a van or station wagon or whatever the big passenger vehicles are called these days. I see 'em up and down the road all the time."

"Fairly common, then. Do *you* own one?"

"Naw. Just got a pick-up and a two-tonner."

"Where were you Wednesday afternoon this week?"

"Wednesday . . . let's see. I think that was the day I took some cows to market. No. No, it wasn't. That was Tuesday. I remember now. I hauled logs to North Garden Wednesday. I got receipts in the truck, if you need proof."

"Not necessary right now. But you might want to hold on to them."

"No problem. You asking these questions for the same reason as what the deputies said yesterday? About a woman missing from down yonder? At the old Bannister place?"

"That's one reason."

"One reason?"

"Yes. The other is that we've found the body of another woman who went missing the same day."

"My God, man! Where? Who? When? What in the world's going on?" Randy Millard asked rhetorically, in machine-gun fashion.

"The body of Roberta Dumond. Near the ford at Slaytor Creek bridge. This morning."

"Mrs. Dumond! I know her. Used to work a little for her husband. Years ago. A real nice lady. Who's the other woman?"

"A real estate agent. Lauren Michaels."

"From Charlottesville?"

"No. Lovingston."

Shirley Millard had said nothing during the whole exchange. Now she turned from where she had been standing just inside the doorway behind her husband's shoulder and started to walk down the hall.

"Mrs. Millard!" Washburn called, "Just a minute, please."

She stopped but did not turn around.

"Mrs. Millard, can you come out to the porch for a minute?" Washburn asked, rather than commanded. She remained motionless.

"Come on, woman. The man ain't got all day," Randy called out, his voice too genial to sound demanding.

Shirley Millard turned and sort of slunk back to the door, then nudged her husband aside enough to stand against him. She looked at Washburn but did not meet his gaze directly.

"What?" she asked bluntly in a smoke-raspy voice.

"I wasn't ignoring you when I was talking to your husband," Washburn offered politely. "I just needed to hear from you one at a time. Now, what about Wednesday for you? Were you here?"

"Yes."

"All day? Didn't go anywhere?"

"I went to the dumpster."

"Howardsville? In the pick-up?"

"Yeah."

"Did you see anyone you didn't know? A strange van or SUV?"

"I didn't pay attention."

"Okay, then, thank you. If you see or hear anything out of the ordinary, give my office a call, all right? Either of you." He handed Randy Millard his card.

"Sure thing, Mr. Washburn. Is there anything else I can do to help?" Randy inquired, apparently genuinely concerned.

Again Washburn noted the sharp contrast in the two personalities, and wondered what the marriage was like.

"Appreciate your offer. I'll pass your name to the rescue crews. I'm sure they need some relief help. Thank you both for now."

On his way to the next interview, Washburn reviewed his impression of the encounter with the Millards. Something about Shirley Millard bothered him. Was she shy? Bipolar? Retarded? Or just plain mean? For the moment he just couldn't pinpoint what it was about her that niggled at his mind.

The next to last interview of the afternoon added to Washburn's perplexity. A man close to seventy, the minister turned out to be dark, dour, and ungracious, although he looked to be younger than his age. He opened his door to Washburn's knocking, stared at the officer, and greeted him bluntly.

"What can I do for you?"

"Sir, I'm Ned Washburn, investigator with the Nelson sheriff's office. I need to ask you a few questions. May I come in?"

"If you must," the minister grumbled, then held the door open for Washburn to enter. "I suppose your visit has to do with the searching going on up and down the river," he added.

Washburn looked about the room, apparently a regular living room. Clean enough, he thought, but without evidence of warmth or comfort. Sparsely furnished, it was indeed cold. The minister motioned for him to sit in a leather wing chair.

"Mr. Netherdon," Washburn began, only to be ungraciously interrupted.

"It's Reverend Netherdon."

Washburn thought, "Oh boy, this should be interesting!" Outwardly he smiled and crossed his legs, the stance suggesting both comfort and authority.

"It should be phrased '*the* Reverend Mr. Netherdon' or 'the Reverend Clovis Netherdon'—that is, if you are an ordained minister."

"WHAT are you talking about? Of course, I'm an ordained minister! Penecostal." The minister was now puffed up and red-faced, despite his usual swarthy appearance.

"Well, surely then, you should know that the word *reverend* does not mean a rank, like captain, or a profession, like doctor. Rather, the word means *worthy of reverence*—and when used in reference to *someone*, it should be preceeded by *the* and followed by a *full name*."

"I'm not a grammar teacher, officer! Besides, what difference does it make?"

"I doubt that I could make you understand," Washburn returned, factitiously. "But to the point: I came to ask if you've seen an unfamiliar van or SUV along the road here this week? Dark color?"

"No. But you should have noticed that I don't have a clear view of the road."

"I believe that one of our deputies noted that *you* have such a vehicle. Right?"

"Yes."

"What is it?"

"I thought the deputy would have told you. It's a Dodge Durango. Dark blue."

"Right. Did you use it Wednesday?"

"No."

"So you were here all day?"

"No," the minister said, growing more impatient by the minute. "I was in Charlottesville. Most of the day."

"You have another vehicle then? Or you rode with someone else?"

"I have a Ford Escort, too. I drove that Wednesday. Both vehicles are in the back yard, like I told the deputy. He looked at them. You can look, too."

"Did anyone use the Durango Wednesday? Your wife or—"

"Nobody used it! I'm a widower. I live alone! What's wrong with you people, that you don't listen?" *the reverend* hissed.

"All right, then. I think that about does it for today," Washburn said coolly as he stood. "Thank you for your time."

"Well, I'm sorry I can't help you, but I wish you luck with the search," the minister said, getting off his high horse. He rose from his chair, too, and moved to open the door for Washburn to exit.

In the doorway Washburn turned on his heel to face Netherdon up close, startling the man.

"You know Roberta Dumond, don't you?" he asked, recalling Blair's comment about Netherdon's trying to get the pastor's position at her church.

"I've met her."

"Interesting you didn't mention it, considering she's chairperson of her church board, and I understand you applied for a position there."

"You didn't ask," Netherdon retorted.

"I also didn't ask if you knew we found her body this morning!" Washburn blurted, watching Netherdon's expression change as the man huffed a slight expulsion of breath.

"No . . . ah . . . I didn't know . . . I . . ."

"You say you're Penecostal? Mrs. Dumond's church is certainly not that de—"

"I could get a license transfer," Netherdon snapped.

"But you didn't get the job."

"I might *yet.*"

"Dare say? Well, good day, Netherdon!" Washburn said dismissively and walked away dramatically, not bothering to look back.

Getting into his cruiser, Washburn chuckled. "Pompous ass! No wonder he's churchless," he said. "And probably why he's a widower!"

Washburn's last interview was with Bob Herman, president of Riverside Hunt Club, along with several club members. Washburn knew Herman casually, knew his nickname was "Big Buck", apparently coined from his having killed a record number of deer—or *bragging* that he had.

The hunters were waiting impatiently for him at their clubhouse located off Route 626. As he drove up, he noticed that one was target-shooting and a couple others were pacing about restlessly. Big Buck came out to meet him, a tall broad-shouldered man sporting a VanDyke goatee. Also reputed to have a stronger bark than bite, Herman characteristically blurted, "Where the hell you been, man? Can't hang around here waiting for you all day!"

"Sorry, Herman. Other seven interviews ran a little long."

"Aw-ite, man! Water over the dam now. Come on in, let's hear what you got to ask."

Herman preceded Washburn inside. Formerly a residence, the structure was now pared down to basic essentials for a hunt camp. Outside there was no front porch or stoop, and inside at least two walls had been removed to create a long main room. Its functional furnishings included a large wood-burning stove, a long pine table, a dozen or so chairs, a battered leather sofa, a range and refrigerator, and a television set. The scuffed floor was bare. Interestingly, the place was very clean.

"Have a seat," Herman invited, his tone sounding more like a command. "You want the others in here?"

"Yes, please. That'll save time for everyone."

Herman stepped to the door and bellowed, "HEY . . . BOYS . . . INSIDE . . . NOW!"

Once they were all assembled, Herman introduced Washburn. Dan Wallace and Ross Peters, the two hunters who had been pacing outside, acknowledged the introduction, pulled chairs to the table, and sat. The hunter who had been target-shooting, Denny Olsey, leaned against the back of the sofa. Herman stood at the end of the table, one foot planted on a chair.

"Fellas," Washburn began, "as you know already, we're investigating the abduction of two women down here this week—"

"What's that got to do with us—with you wanting to question us?" the sofa-leaning hunter asked.

"We've found the same tire tracks at three places involved—"

"With Mrs. Dumond? Heard you found her this morning," Herman interrupted, his tone softened considerably.

"With her, yes," Washburn answered, looking up at Herman, "but also at the property where the real estate woman disappeared from."

"So you figure the two women are connected?" asked Ross Peters from his position at the table.

"Not the women themselves. But what happened to them, yes. At least their abductions. We don't know if the real estate woman is dead or still alive."

"Who's the real estate woman? A friend of mine is in real estate . . ." Herman trailed off, shaken suddenly by a possibility he hadn't considered before.

"Lauren Michaels, with Town Mountain Realty in Lovingston," Washburn responded.

"My friend's an owner of that company. Blair Camfield. I've got to phone her . . ." Herman mumbled, sighing with relief that the missing woman was not Blair. He and his wife Betty had been away on a business trip the previous week, returning home only the evening before. He had heard the news about Roberta Dumond only when the sheriff's office called to arrange this interview today.

"Back to my question, Officer Washburn, why do you want to question us?" the sofa-leaning Olsey asked.

"As I said, we've found tire tracks, size 265/70 R 16 or close to that. Anyway, like the size used on a lot of large pick-ups, vans, and SUV's. I expect that most of your members drive such vehicles—"

"Are you implying that one of us had something to do—" Olsey bristled.

"Hold on, Olsey," Herman cut in. "Washburn's not accusing anybody. Least not yet. Are you?" he challenged Washburn.

"Of course not. Process of elimination. We're checking out tires on such vehicles all the way from Buffalo Station, west of Norwood, all the way east to just this side of Scottsville. Don't want to discriminate by leaving out vehicles regularly driven in this area but whose owners live elsewhere. Like some of your members—"

"Aw-ite, dammit, we get it! You tell whoever's gonna do the checking to be at Wingina Store tomorrow morning at 7:00. Sharp! I'll have the whole membership there with their hunting vehicles. Now, if you don't mind, the four of us would like to get outta here and do some searching on our own. Whole lot of logging roads in the hunt country between here and Howardsville—and we know nearly every foot of them!"

"Good idea. Appreciate your help. However," Washburn cautioned, "if you find her alive, don't tell her about Mrs. Dumond. Leave that to me. And don't do anything to contaminate a crime scene," he added as he got up and moved toward the door. "Give me a minute out here. I want to snap some shots of your tires before you get going."

Herman snorted. "Figured as much. No problem."

Washburn checked to see if all four tires on a vehicle had the same tread, then took a Polaroid shot of just one tire. On the back of each of the four pictures he stuck a white label and wrote on it the vehicle's VIN, license number, and owner's name.

"Thanks, fellas," Washburn called out as he finished the labeling and slid behind the wheel of his cruiser. "Keep in touch," he added, and waved good-bye.

Big Buck Herman watched Washburn drive out toward the highway, then reached into his truck for his cell phone.

"Hold on a sec," he called to his three fellow hunters. "Just gotta make a quick call," he added. And dialed Blair Camfield's number.

He told Blair that he had just learned about her sales rep, offered expressions of hope, said that he and some of his hunting buddies were beginning their own search for Lauren, and promised they wouldn't give up until they found her.

When he finished the conversation with Blair, he phoned several other hunters and gave directions to where they were to join him, Olsey, Wallace, and Peters. He issued brief instructions to the three men with him before roaring out of the parking area to initiate what came to be tagged the "Hunters Team" search efforts.

At 6:00 near a place in the forest known as "The Crossroads", Dan Wallace, widely known as a sharp tracker, found a tire tread mark that was far too fresh to have been made by hunters during the previous year's deer season—or during the spring turkey season. He cell-phoned Herman to join him for a look. Herman snapped a couple pictures with his digital camera, which he would print on his computer when he returned home. Peters found a broken parking-light lens beside a fallen tree that was lying partly in a logging trail leading to "The Crossroads". He phoned Herman, too, to come take pictures before he picked up the lens.

That activity ended the hunters' searching for the day. By 7:00 it was too dark to continue in the woods. They agreed to resume their search Sunday morning-after the "tire examination".

ELEVEN

At 9:00 Sunday morning, Big Buck Herman and thirty-five hunt club members set out to traverse a five-square-mile grid. Several men had brought their hound dogs along. The forested area was criss-crossed with numerous driveable old logging roads and some trails too overgrown for vehicular travel. Eight hunters assembled at "The Crossroads", parked their vehicles, and paired off in two's to walk along both sides of four roads, paralleling a road ten feet inside the woods. If there was a body to be found, living or dead, they figured it would not be in the middle of the road.

Each hunter had a cell phone, along with a list of numbers for the cell phones of other hunters in the group scattered throughout the grid.

Two hours later Herman and his partner, Ross Peters, along with Herman's hound dog "Ralph", found tire tracks leading into and out of a small branch. Herman noted that the tracks matched the ones in the photos he'd taken the day before. The two men and dog continued to walk off-road, while keeping eyes on the roadway. A half-mile farther along they reached the lower side of an overgrown field, the remains of a long-abandoned homestead. The shed portion and vine-covered stone chimney of a burned-down house stood at the top of a low hill. Hunters knew the place as "Broken-Top Chestnut", a name going back to the 1930's and derived from the presence of a chestnut tree whose top portion had been snapped off during a storm. All that remained of the tree was an eight-foot stump covered with vines.

"Look here," Ross Peters called back to Herman from what had been the front yard.

"What you got?" Herman asked, huffing and puffing as he climbed the last few feet to the yard. His hunting was done mostly from the side of a pick-up truck or on an ATV, not tracking game on foot. Clearly he was not in the best physical condition.

"Same tire tracks in this bare area. And looks like the vehicle was turned around right over there," Peters said, pointing to a small scrub pine with broken branches located near one side of the shed.

"Yep. You're right. Let's check the shed," Herman directed.

What had been a doorway from the shed into the main house was now solidly boarded over, leaving no entrance on the front. Ralph ran ahead to the backside of the structure, put his front paws up on the door there, and began whining. Herman and Peters were still twenty feet away when they heard a voice. Not very strong, but strong enough to reach their ears.

"Help," it said simply. Feebly. At the sound Ralph jumped up and down on all fours, yet managed to paw the door furiously.

They sprinted to the door. "Who's there?" Herman bellowed.

"Lauren Michaels," came the weak reply.

"You alone?" Peters asked. Herman glared at him.

"Yes."

"What you scared of, man?" Herman hissed at Peters. "Hold on, girl! We're gonna get you out! Hey, we're local hunters! Don't be scared." Bob Herman was so excited, so nervous, that he didn't realize how jumbled his statements sounded.

A four-foot-long, two-by-six-inch board stretched across the door, its ends resting in steel brackets on each side of the door, firmly sealing Lauren inside. Herman lifted the board, and Peters pulled open the heavy door. It squeaked on rusted hinges.

Disheveled and dirty, Lauren stumbled to the opening and grabbed the door frame to steady herself. She squinted as bright sunlight hit her eyes. "If I weren't so filthy, I'd hug you!" she said hoarsely, smiling at the two men while tears streaked her face.

"Never mind that, gal. Come here," Herman commanded gruffly, holding out his arms and trying hard to hide his emotions. He folded Lauren into a bear hug. Peters patted her shoulder awkwardly. Ralph licked her hand and leaned against her legs.

Herman continued to hold Lauren, quietly shushing her sobs. Peters stepped away and whipped out his phone.

"You okay?" Herman asked Lauren, leaning back to scrutinize her face.

"I think so. But this still hurts," she answered, and touched a finger lightly to the back of her head.

Herman turned her head gently sideways and looked at the back. The hair was matted with dried blood, but he thought he could see a portion of cut flesh.

"Where *is* this place?" Lauren asked, glancing at the surroundings.

"Timber company land, maybe ten miles from where you were abducted. Known for years as Broken-Top Chestnut."

"Hey Olsey, who's closest to the vehicles at The Crossroads?" Peters called loudly into his phone.

"Blunt, I think. He doubled back a little while ago. Why?" Olsey answered.

"We need a vehicle brought to Broken Top—and whatever snacks any of you have. Also water. Call Blunt, okay?"

"Sure. Ya'll in trouble?"

"Hell no, man! We found her! ALIVE."

"Hallelujah! Well, all right! I'll get Blunt. And I'm on the way to get my Jeep, too. Be right there!"

"Come on, Lauren, I'll help you to that boulder over there. You can sit while we wait. Help'll be here in a jiffy," Herman promised. He removed his lightweight hunting coat and put it around her shoulders.

"Thank you. Good idea, too, to get farther from the stink!" Lauren said, trying to joke about the stench of her three and a half days' imprisonment in the small building. As soon as Herman lowered her to the boulder, Ralph sat beside her, licked her cheek, then sank to his haunches and laid his head in her lap.

Herman removed a phone from an inside pocket of his shell vest and dialed a number. "May I speak to Ned Washburn," he said to the person who answered, and waited a few seconds for Washburn to pick up. "Hey, tell him it's one of the searchers!" he prompted loudly.

"Washburn here," came the immediate response.

"Officer, this is Bob Herman. We've found Ms. Michaels."

"A___live?" Washburn asked, his voice tentative.

"Very!"

"Great! Her condition?"

"Tired, weak . . . hungry . . . a little dirty. Got a wound on the back of her head. Not too serious, I hope."

"Where are you, Herman?"

Big Buck Herman described the area. "Drive a four-by-four. And ask a rescue squad unit to follow you. I'll post a hunter on Route 626 at the entrance of a logging road. He'll lead you to us."

"Fine. Evidence—"

"We haven't disturbed a damn thing!"

"I didn't mean—"

"Never mind. Look, just hurry, okay? Meanwhile, I'm gonna call Blair Camfield."

"Good. Tell her to meet me at the intersection of Routes 56 and 626 in . . . oh, about twenty minutes. I'll pick her up and bring her along. And tell Ms. Michaels that I'll call her daughter Page."

Herman rang off and dialed Blair. He knew she would be home. She was too upset about Lauren and Roberta Dumond to attend church this day. What he didn't know was that there would be no service at Blair's church. Mrs. Dumond had disappeared before she could arrange for a substitute minister to conduct the Sunday service.

Ross Peters and Big Buck divided the list of phone numbers and dialed to tell the remaining thirty-two hunters the news, thus calling off their search efforts, and to tell them to re-assemble at the club house.

"Pick up some lunch stuff in Howardsville, enough for all of us, charge it to my account, and make coffee when you get to the club," Herman instructed the last two hunters he called, two of the eight who had fanned out in an area closer to Howardsville. "The rest of us'll be along in a little while. Soon's the investigator and rescue squad get here."

Just as Herman rang off, a Jeep Cherokee and a Ford pick-up entered the overgrown field and started to roar up the hill.

"Ross! Keep 'em off the tire track and broken scrub!" Herman yelled. Peters ran to the area and signaled the drivers to veer away.

Denny Olsey and Willard Blunt rolled from their vehicles, carrying snacks, two bottles of water, and a roll of paper towels. "Hello, ma'am," they greeted Lauren, both grinning foolishly, happily. "We brought you a snack," Blunt added, boyishly.

"Oh, thank you!" Lauren exclaimed, and smiled sweetly at the two men as she reached greedily for the food.

"Hold it!" Herman barked. He reached for the paper towels, yanked off several sheets and dampened them with a little water from a bottle he snatched out of Olsey's hand. Then he wiped Lauren's face as gently as if she were a baby. Afterward he handed her the wet towels to clean her hands.

"Now give her what you have," Herman said, standing back.

The two hunters had managed to scavenge only two doughnuts, a Snickers bar, and a banana from vehicles back at "The Crossroads". Lauren devoured all of it gratefully, washing it down with a bottle of water.

"Best meal I've ever had! You four guys are my best friends forever," Lauren exuded, despite her weakened condition, then teared-up again. "That's for sure!"

Denny Olsey, who considered himself something of a ladies man, took a seat beside Lauren on the boulder. And she took notice! Admittedly, he was a good-looking hunk—tall, athletically built, with curly hair and twinkling blue eyes.

They all engaged in small talk until Washburn, led by a hunter driving a beat-up four-by-four truck, arrived in an old black Chevvy Blazer with faded ID on its doors. Deputy Taskell and Blair were riding with him. A rescue unit followed closely. Again, Peters signaled for the vehicles to avoid running over the tire track and damaged scrub pine. The beat-up lead truck turned around and left.

Blair accepted Washburn's assistance to descend from the back seat, then with the use of one crutch she hobbled as quickly as she could toward the rear of the shack. She saw Bob Herman first. "You *said* you'd find her! Thank you, Bob," she said and hugged him. Ralph rubbed against her good leg. She bent to pat him.

"Ralph helped, too," Bob "Big Buck" Herman bragged proudly.

Lauren rose feebly and took a step or two forward when she saw Blair. "Oh, Lauren!" Blair cried, then dropped the crutch and threw her arms around her friend. Tears streaming the cheeks of both women, they wobbled slightly then lurched sideways. Olsey and Herman lunged to grab them, keeping them from falling to the ground. Olsey steadied Lauren back to a sitting position on the boulder, then motioned Blair to join her.

"Deputy Taskell, will you fetch my carry-all from the back seat?" Blair requested.

Then she faced Lauren. "What in the world happened? Are you badly hurt?" she asked anxiously.

"I'm okay now, thanks to my saviours here," Lauren answered, smiling as she indicated Herman and Peters, the latter just rounding the shack on his return. "And to these two who brought food for my starving body," she added, acknowledging Olsey and Blunt.

"Shucks, it wasn't much," Blunt injected, self-consciously scuffing the toe of his boot against a clump of dead grass.

A young man and a middle-aged woman, both wearing jackets with Nelson Rescue Squad emblazoned on the backs, pushed past the onlookers to get to Lauren. They gave her a peripheral examination, checking vital signs and taking temperature, etc., reporting that she was obviously dehydrated. They inspected the head wound, pronounced the need for antibiotic dressing and stitches, and recommended that Lauren be taken to the medical center. Otherwise, they ruled her condition to be fair.

"I have something for you," Blair said when the rescue people said good-bye and left. She signaled Deputy Taskell to approach with her canvas carry-all bag. He handed it to her. She reached in and withdrew a thermos bottle and a tube of styrofoam cups. "Figured you could use some of this."

Blair poured coffee into a cup and handed it to Lauren. She knew Lauren took it black and unsweetened.

"Oh, I've gone to heaven!" Lauren exclaimed after taking a sip.

"And here're chicken salad sandwiches and chips," Blair offered.

"Thanks, but I think I'll hold off on eating more for a bit. Don't want to overeat and get sick. I'd like to keep your food for later, though."

"Of course. Please do. By the way, I rang Page. She said that Officer Washburn had called her already. So she knows you've been found. Alive. NOW, tell us what happened Wednesday . . . we've been worried sick . . . been looking and looking . . ." Blair prodded.

"Frankly, I don't know. I remember walking down to a shed behind the Bannister house after the customer left. Incidentally, he wasn't interested in the property," Lauren interjected, but quickly resumed her story when she saw impatience flare in Blair's eyes. "The shed door was open, and I intended to close it. Out of curiosity, though, I stepped inside. Immediately I felt a splitting pain in my head. That was it. The next thing I was aware of was waking up in that shack over there. As best I could see my watch, it was 6:30 then—not dark outside but only a little light coming through cracks to the inside. I had no idea where I was or why. I pushed against the door, to no avail, of course. Then I felt around, absurdly thinking my purse might be there and I could get to my cell phone. I tried to move around but got dizzy and stumbled over crates and junk. So finally I just settled down in a corner, rested my back against the wall, and waited for someone to find me. Or just for morning. You must know the rest. Mornings came and nights went . . . for what? . . . three . . . no, four days, if today is indeed Sunday."

"And you didn't see anyone? Hear anything?" Washburn questioned.

"No. Only birds by day—and rodents by night!" Lauren shuddered, recalling both kinds of sounds which she hated.

"Didn't see or *hear* a vehicle?"

"No. Nothing. Nothing human."

"So, nobody's returned since Wednesday," Washburn reflected. "Huumm . . ." He was thinking that it certainly appeared she had been left there to die. "Okay. Enough for now. You've experienced quite an ordeal. I'm going to send you and Blair out by one of these hunters, back to Blair's car. I'll want to talk to you some more later, though. Okay?"

Lauren nodded affirmatively.

"Which of you fellas—"

"I'll take 'em, Officer," Osley interrupted to volunteer. "I've got more room in the Jeep," he elaborated quickly, then blushed. His interest in Lauren appeared to be more than a desire to help a crime victim. Certainly long gone was the adamant attitude he had displayed during Washburn's interview the day before.

"Fine. Taskell, would you help Olsey lift Lauren to his Jeep? Herman and I'll help Blair. You other two fellas bring along the canvas bag, bottles, and whatever, okay?"

They made their way to the front yard as a group. Lauren and Blair were deposited in the Jeep; Herman, Peters, and Blunt said their good-bye's to Lauren and then piled into Blunt's truck, with the hound dog Ralph riding on the back.

"Talk to you later, Blair," Herman called from the truck's open window. Blair waved and blew him a kiss.

Washburn touched her arm lightly. "Thanks," he said, keeping his voice low. "Take care of Lauren. But let me tell her about the . . . the *other*. Okay?" Blair nodded. "I'll call you later and fill you in about yesterday's interviews," he finished.

She smiled at him but blew no kiss.

Washburn and Deputy Taskell remained behind to inspect the crime scene, take photos, dust for prints, and make molds of tracks.

Denny Olsey parked his Jeep beside Blair's Olds sedan, on the passenger side. Behavior contrasting his rough appearance in rumpled much-worn hunter's attire and facial two-day stubble, Olsey moved swiftly around his vehicle and chivalrously opened the front passenger door for Lauren.

"Help you, too, in just a sec, Mrs. Camfield," he said as he grasped Lauren's elbow and assisted her transfer to Blair's car.

He repeated the effort with Blair. When she was positioned behind the steering wheel, he deposited her crutch in the back seat and shut her door.

Blair lowered her window. "Thank you, Denny, for your help. We really appreciate it," Blair said.

"Glad to do it . . . been concerned . . . uh, I'll check on ya'll later," he finished, suddenly awkward with self-consciousness.

"That will be nice," Lauren acknowledged, smiling sweetly at him. "Good-bye. For *now.*" Her near tragic experience apparently had not hindered her flirtatiousness.

Both Blair and Lauren waved to Olsey as they turned into the highway. He waved back. And continued to watch the car until it sped from sight.

"Think he's attracted to you, Lauren," Blair teased.

"I don't see how he could be! As filthy as I am! Don't see how anyone can stand the odor. In fact, I'm stinking up your car as well as his Jeep!"

"Oh, Lauren, that's nothing. Absolutely nothing. We all see past stuff like that. Besides, it's not as obvious as you think. Please don't let it embarrass you. Shoot, a little soap and water will make you and the cars good as new!" Blair finished, laughing, trying to lighten the atmosphere.

"He is kind of good-looking—in an outdoorsy way. Shaved and dressed casually, he might even be handsome," Lauren ventured.

"See? You might actually get something *good* out of this adventure!" Blair laughed. When she heard no response, she glanced at Lauren—and quickly apologized for her flippancy. "I'm sorry."

"That's okay, Blair. But adventure it surely was not! More like a trip to hell. Oh, I was *so scared* after the first day! By today I was having to accept the fact that no one would find me in time . . ." Lauren broke off, choking on tears.

Blair slowed the car and grasped one of Lauren's hands. She was too choked up to speak herself. They rode in silence the rest of the way to Lovingston.

Only when Blair stopped briefly at the realty office did Lauren speak again. "Where's my SUV? Or was it stolen?" she asked, alarmed when she realized that the Suzuki was not on the office lot.

"It's okay! Impounded at the sheriff's office. Searchers found it in the woods about a quarter mile behind the Bannister house—fortunately not damaged. And your purse and cell phone were still on the passenger seat, undisturbed, along with your file folder."

Lauren exhaled loudly. "This thing's getting stranger all the time," she mused.

"How so?"

"Well, I wasn't raped, my car and stuff weren't stolen. I mean, why was I knocked unconscious and moved nearly a dozen miles to that shack? And just left there? It's strange. There's no apparent reason. Mr. Earndahl seemed so nice, a gentle person. Don't see what possible motive . . ." Lauren stopped suddenly. "My God! Has *he* been arrested?" she blurted.

"No, no. He didn't do it, Lauren. His time is accounted for. Besides, his car tires wouldn't be a match for the tracks found at the Bannister shed and at the shack where you were found."

"Oh." Lauren gazed out the window for a bit, trying to absorb, to reflect. "SO . . . somebody else. Huumm. Well, I'm glad it wasn't Mr. Earndahl, that my impression of him was right."

Blair drove Lauren to the medical center and stayed with her while the doctor on duty examined the head wound and followed up with vision tests and observations of Lauren's movements and responses. When the doctor seemed satisfied that Lauren revealed no evidence of critical injury, she cut away a narrow strip of hair, washed the head wound with an antiseptic preparation, and dried it. Then, after injecting a mild dose of anesthetic to dull pain, she deftly sutured the abrasion and applied a topical antibiotic.

"Don't bend over for more than a moment, don't lift anything heavier than ten pounds," she admonished Lauren. "Come back in two days for me to have a look. And don't wash your hair before then," she added.

From the medical center, Blair took Lauren straight home. She prepared hot tea in the kitchen while Page sat in the bathroom to monitor her mother's showering. Once Lauren emerged wrapped in a clean terrycloth robe and was ensconced in a family-room recliner, with a cup of hot tea on a TV table beside her, Blair felt comfortable about leaving her. She knew that Page was competent to attend Lauren's needs for the following few days. Meredith, the neighbor and friend, would help, too.

Meanwhile, after lunching and sharing the day's experiences with the other hunters back at the hunt club's camp, Bob Herman, accompanied by Ross Peters, went to his home near Wingina to log on. He figured he might be able to get a lead on the source of the parking light lens that Ross had found the evening before.

An hour after booting up his computer and going to numerous web sites featuring old and new vehicle parts, especially for SUV's and pick-up trucks, he had gotten nowhere. Hating to concede that he was lacking in research skills, finally he had to ask his wife Betty for help. With flashing finger work on the keyboard and precision mousing and clicking of the cursor, she quickly pulled up displays of the front ends of full-size SUV models for the past five years. In short order she had a hit. The digital photo of the lens found in the woods matched the parking light lens pictured on the Dodge Durango, a model basically unchanged for the previous several years.

"Damn!" Big Buck blurted, and jumped up from his chair.

"What is it, Bob?" Betty Herman asked, her mouth pinched with concern.

"Netherdon! He's got a Durango. And he sure has a grudge against Roberta Dumond. HAD a grudge," he corrected, exaggerating the *had.*

"He's a minister! Surely you don't think he's involved in these—"

"I sure wouldn't put it past him!" Herman said emphatically, overriding his wife's words. "Never could stand the son of a—"

"BOB!" his wife cut him off. "No cursing, remember," she cautioned.

"Well, he is one! Sneaky bas . . . buzzard, too. I wouldn't trust him as far as I could throw him."

"He *was* pretty upset about not getting to be pastor of Roberta Dumond's church down yonder. He told our minister he'd been done dirty," Ross Peters pointed out.

Ross was a member of a predominantly black Baptist church in another community in the county.

"What're you going to do?" Betty asked nervously.

"Going to see him. Find out—"

"Bob, your temper! Do you think it's wise to confront him? After all—"

"Look, I'm not gonna attack him! Even though somebody ought to beat the sh . . . shucks out of him. I just want to ask him some questions . . . see his face. If it'll make you feel better, Betty, I'll take Ross here along. Okay with you, Ross?"

"Uh . . . sure."

"Well, please, please be careful," Betty pleaded as she walked behind them to the door.

On the drive to the minister's home, Ross Peters started having second thoughts. He had once seen Herman raging at a hunter from another club, a man who had ventured onto Herman's leased hunting land with six deer hounds. The confrontation had not been a pretty sight.

"What's your plan, Big Buck?" he queried.

"Dunno. Exactly. Ask to see the Durango probably."

"Don't you reckon the deputies have looked at it already?"

"Even so, buddy, they don't know we found the broken lens."

"Wasn't thinking of that. You're right. They wouldn't of known to check for a damaged light. Just looking at tire treads . . ." Ross trailed off, momentarily lost in thought.

"Ross, in case you're worried, I'm not looking for trouble. Don't plan to hurt anybody, understand. Just trying to help find out who did these terrible things. And why."

"I understand," Ross responded quickly. But he didn't understand, and his sense of worry was not alleviated. He really had no idea why it was *he* and *Herman* going to see the minister; he felt they should be giving their information to the sheriff or his investigator instead. He feared that Big Buck might have an ax to grind, so to speak, and that the visit could somehow backfire.

They arrived at Netherdon's house in late afternoon. Before they could get out of Herman's pick-up, Clovis Netherdon walked out onto his front porch to intercept them. He leaned against the railing, his arms folded across his chest. It was a defiant stance.

"How may I help you, gentlemen?" he called brusquely across the space of forty yards. He had not yet recognized that it was Big Buck Herman, and he had never met Ross Peters.

"Afternoon, Rev," Big Buck greeted the minister, his use of 'Rev' clearly conveying his lack of respect for the man.

"Oh, it's you, Herman. Didn't recognize you right off. As I said, how may I help you?"

"Your SUV. Mind if I take a look at it?"

"Why? I wasn't thinking to sell it."

"Just curious about a Durango. You mind?"

"Suit yourself. It's around back. On second thought, I'll go with you."

The three men walked around the house to the back yard. The dark blue vehicle, parked near a huge maple tree, was shiny clean—looking as if it had just been washed and waxed.

Big Buck walked slowly around the SUV, scrutinizing details. When he had completely circled it, he stood in front of the grill, his expression registering puzzlement.

"Satisfied?" the minister asked, watching Herman suspicously.

"Yeah, I guess. Not what I had in mind, though. But thanks," Big Buck said and retreated a few steps. Then he turned back abruptly. "You know Lauren Michaels, Rev?"

"WHAT?" Netherdon snapped. "What are you suggesting, Herman?"

"Nothing. In particular. She's a right attractive woman, and I know you like women. Thought you might have seen her down here the other day—"

"How dare you slander me! Look, you . . . you . . . poor excuse of a person! Get off my property *now*! This very minute! Or I'll call the cops."

"Why so angry, Rev?" Big Buck taunted.

"OFF! NOW!" the minister shouted, face red, mouth sputtering, fists clenched, body shaking as he rocked back and forth on his heels. Ross Peters thought the man was on the verge of having a stroke. Big Buck laughed, enjoying the spectacle.

"Okay, okay, cool it. We're leaving," Bib Buck said and smiled benevolently, mockingly. "Try to behave yourself, hear," he called over his shoulder, walking briskly back to his pick-up. Ross Peters was fast on his tracks. He had said not a single word during the confrontation between the two men.

Back in the truck he turned to Herman. "The lens won't broke. Why'd you goad him, Big Buck?"

"No reason. Except I enjoy it. See, he's a first class hypocrite—selfish, not compassionate or kind or loving—just the opposite of what a minister should be. I can't stand frauds like him. And I guess *I* just have to let him know how I feel because most people are too kind to tell him to his face what they really think of him."

"I thought he was going to have a stroke. It was kinda scary," Peters confessed.

"Hell, he's too mean to die!" Big Buck asserted playfully.

"What now?" Peters inquired when they were back on the public road.

"Let's drive into Lovingston, give the lens and the pictures we've taken to Ned Washburn. And tell him maybe old Netherdon should be investigated some more. I smelled a rat there!"

TWELVE

Blair eased herself down into Richard's chair and pushed back to a semi-reclining position. Her wine glass sat beside her on a lamp table. She lighted a cigarette. And sighed. It was heaven to be off her feet and alone, supported by wine and a cig. An exhausting day this Sunday had been, and it wasn't ended yet at six o'clock. Thankfully, but uncharacteristically sensitive to her feelings, Richard had volunteered to take the children to Lynchburg for pizza and a movie. She was utterly submerged in solitude, yet she was filled with anxiety. Anxiety for the ongoing investigation, Lauren's trauma, pending confrontations—especially the one with Ned Washburn that would surely be necessary soon.

"Again, as Scarlet might say, 'I'll just think about all that tomorrow'," she para-quoted, causing two dogs to raise their heads and look at her in puzzlement. She smiled. "You think your mistress is crazy, don't you? Frankly, you might have a point there!" she added, mocking herself, and took a big sip of wine.

The phone on the lamp table jangled, almost causing her to spill wine down the front of her sweatshirt.

"Hello."

"It's Ned."

"Hey," she returned, immediately irritated with herself for the girlish, conspiratorial tone of her voice. But she couldn't deny the rush of warmth that pervaded her body.

Washburn cleared his throat and proceeded to report Saturday's interviews and other aspects of the investigation of Roberta Dumond's death and Lauren's abduction.

"Fingerprint analysts didn't find a match for the print lifted from the latch on the shed door. Said that it appeared to be from a small hand. Could be from somebody looking at the property, and mean nothing. Then Bob Herman came by this afternoon. Gave me a broken parking light lens and some pictures of tire tracks that he and his hunt pals took on one of the logging roads. The tracks match those photographed at the Bannister property, at Slaytor Creek ford, and at the shack where Lauren was found. Also match those in the photo you took at Roberta Dumond's home."

"Has your investigation turned up a vehicle with tires that match the prints?"

"Yes. Several. None belonging to the hunters, though, thank goodness."

"Several? Whose?"

"Actually we found ten vehicles with that tire design, but ruled out seven—"

"Ruled out? On what basis?"

"Four have owners and drivers with sound alibis for Wednesday. One is size seventeen. Two have tires with too much wear on the treads. So we're left with three that fit."

"Who're the owners?"

"A power company lineman from Scottsville, a factory worker from near Esmont, and a minister from—"

"A minister? Who?"

"Clovis Netherdon."

"Oh my God!"

"What?"

"Bob Herman—Big Buck—*said* Netherdon is involved somehow! And I thought Bob was just saying that because he doesn't like the man."

"Yeah, he just told me he thought Netherdon should be investigated further."

"Did he tell you he went to Netherdon's house this afternoon and had some kind of confrontation?"

"No. But it doesn't surprise me. Herman feels very strongly about what's happened down there."

"Yes, he certainly does. And especially as a good friend of mine, he wants to be helpful . . . on my behalf . . . because Lauren and Bert are my friends . . ." Blair trailed off, reminding herself that Roberta Dumond could no longer be referred to in the present tense.

"You okay?" Washburn asked gently.

"Yes . . . yes . . . really, I am. But it's all finally beginning to sink in. And all so sad, so wasteful. I just feel so . . . so, I don't know . . . flat . . . drained, I suppose."

"I can imagine. Is there anything I can do?"

His words were like arms embracing her, his voice like a caress. Blair felt herself responding, sinking. Then she caught herself just before speaking—and probably revealing her response. "Watch it, Camfield," she cautioned herself in thought.

"No . . . no. But thank you, Ned. Just keep investigating, that's all. What's next? Do *you* think Netherdon is involved? I've heard he was awfully upset with Bert about being turned down for the pastorship, but . . . I mean, that's got nothing to do with Lauren—"

Washburn interrupted. "Could be an accidental connection of some sort. Rather than a *planned* connection. At any rate, we're looking further. Be assured that we'll leave no stone unturned!"

"I know . . . I know."

"Will you be in Lovingston tomorrow?"

"At my office, yes. Got lots of stuff to catch up on there. And planning to do for Bert's funeral service. I'm helping Della."

Washburn didn't hear in her answer any opening, any invitation, for him to meet with her. "I see," he said as matter-of-factly as he could manage. "Well, take care."

"You, too," Blair whispered, her tone intimate, despite her earlier resolve to exercise self-control.

She hung up abruptly, almost dropping the phone on its base, and exhaled loudly. Drained her wine glass. Then glanced at her watch.

"Damn!" She had planned to go to Bert's house to discuss with Della some details for the funeral service. "But I can't . . . I just can't . . . not now . . . not tonight!" she announced dramatically to the empty room. Five dogs wagged their tails and turned doleful eyes to their mistress.

Blair could have dealt with Della alone, but she knew the clutch of church women would be there, too, and her emotions were far too raw for such public exposure. One had to be in very good form in order to protect one's vulnerability from that gaggle!

"It can wait 'til tomorrow," she finished, and struggled out of the big recliner to go refill her wine glass.

At 9:00 Sunday night Washburn sat at his office desk, trying to concentrate on finishing a list of the next steps to take in the investigation. After his conversation with Blair, he and Sheriff Oakley had spent nearly two hours discussing the case and examining evidence collected to date. They had agreed that Clovis Netherdon warranted further investigation. Consequently, Netherdon was at the top of the list. He would get another visit first thing Monday morning.

Washburn made a final note, then rolled his chair a little away from the desk, crossed his legs, cupped his hands behind his head, and leaned back. He closed his eyes in order to visualize Blair's face. And reflect. When, he asked himself, had he *first* felt attracted to her? Was it Thursday when she had accompanied him to the Bannister property? No, before. Was it the night before that when she had reported Lauren missing? No, before. Much before. Truth be told—well, acknowledged now to himself—he had felt an attraction the year before when she and her business partner, Landis Galleher, had involved themselves in the investigation of a murder that occurred in a house which they had for sale. Felt it, yes, but had done nothing to show it—or even to acknowledge it to himself at the time, he realized now. For one thing, their encounters had been brief and never alone. And, more significant, at the time his emotional energy had been devoted to imploring his wife to reconcile, to not pursue a divorce. Ironically, it had been Landis back then whom he sought out to confide in and from whom to solicit advice. None of his efforts had succeeded, however. In late November, four weeks after an arrest was made in the open-house murder case, his wife officially filed for divorce. He was thirty-six, childless, and devasted. During the year following he had buried himself in work more than ever, in teaching a class at Piedmont Community College, and in assisting with local youth activities. When he had time off from police work and no activities scheduled, he alternated visits to his parents in Winchester with fishing trips arranged by law enforcement friends, solo trips to museums and historic sites, and recreational piloting. His path had not crossed Blair's again until Wednesday night.

Now he was hooked, smitten. She was in his thoughts constantly. He found that her playfulness, bold outspokenness, and intense drive to help others, balanced by her sensitivity and strong sensuality, rendered her an interesting and exciting personality. She was lithely graceful yet athletic—tall and very attractive. All together, she was a package that he found intriguing and irresistible.

And probably out of reach. Or was she? Surely he wasn't mistaken that she was attracted to him in return. But obviously she was conflicted, torn. After all, she was married. She had two children. She was too honest, too caring to abandon her responsibilities. Wasn't she?

And, thus, he found himself back to block one: What to do? Avoid her in order to squelch his feelings—or try to? Throw caution to the winds and just let her know how he felt? Chance reciprocation or risk rejection? Almost certainly subject her to stronger conflict—even hurt?

"What a helluva choice!" Washburn lamented, springing to an upright position and walking the chair back to his desk. Then he stood, picked up several file folders, moved to the door, flicked the light switch, and snapped the door shut with force.

THIRTEEN

With search warrant in hand, Washburn and two deputies, Joe Brown and Orieman Taskell, descended upon Clovis Nehterdon's property Monday at noon.

"You're here again, officers? Whatever for this time?" Netherdon greeted them on his front porch.

Washburn handed the warrant to the minister. "To search your Durango. And house, too, possibly. We'll start with the vehicle," he announced.

"WHAT is going on? I had nothing—absolutely nothing—to do with the murder and abduction. I have TOLD you so before!" the minister shouted.

"Tire treads matching those on your Durango and two other vehicles were found at four places involving the crimes."

"Four places! Impossible! Has to be one of the others. I didn't even drive the Durango last week!" Netherdon sputtered.

"Then you have nothing to fear, sir. However, we have to search your SUV. As well as the other two vehicles."

"Go ahead! You won't find a thing!" Netherdon barked.

The three officers donned plastic gloves and began the search. Several minutes later Deputy Joe Brown, checking out the cargo area, called to Washburn.

"Captain, got something," he said, pointing to the latch on the spare tire well-cover.

"What'dya see?"

"Hair . . . maybe several strands," Deputy Brown answered.

"Good work. Bag it. See any stains back there?"

"Looks recently vacuumed. But one area of carpet is darker."

"Nothing apparent on the back seat," Washburn reported. "What about up front, Orie?" he asked.

"Don't see anything yet, Captain," Deputy Taskell replied, "but I just thought of something," he continued as he turned from the front seat and started walking to the rear of the vehicle.

"Move over a little, Joe," he directed Deputy Brown when he reached the opened hatch. Washburn delayed Taskell long enough for them to study the carpet cursorily.

When Joe Brown moved back a couple steps, Deputy Taskell leaned into the cargo area and lifted the spare tire well-cover. "Uh-huh!" he exclaimed. "Thought so!"

"Thought what?" Washburn and Brown asked simultaneously.

"The tire iron is missing."

"Well, that does it!" Washburn blurted. "We're impounding this thing. Hard to tell what else the forensics guys might flesh out. Call for a roll-back to pick it up, Joe. I'll go tell the minister."

When Washburn finished his explanation for impounding the Durango, Netherdon's face was red with fury.

"What do you mean, found evidence? Evidence of what? I tell you once again: I *didn't* drive the Durango all last week! This is utter harrassment! I'm calling a lawyer. Right now!" he snapped, whirling about to re-enter his house.

"You do that, sir," Washburn returned. "We'll be in touch with you as soon as the forensics team finishes with your vehicle," he added as he descended the porch steps.

On Tuesday the lab report on the "red" hair was faxed to the sheriff's office.

"Ned, here's the test report on that hair you recovered from Mrs. Dumond's body," Sheriff Oakley said as he handed the paper to Washburn. "Human hair with a bad dye job is all it tells us now. But down the road it might be crucial. By the way, how did the boys do with the searches of those other two vehicles?"

"Clean."

"Case against the minister getting tighter then."

"Yep. Hair and blood tests could cinch it."

"No doubt. Well, I've got a meeting in Charlottesville. You need anything from there?"

"Yeah, but I need to do it myself. Some interviewing, that is."

"Well, then, see you later." And with that, the sheriff moved noiselessly back to his own office.

Washburn phoned the church division superintendent's office and arranged an appointment for 2:00 that afternoon.

"What can I do to help, officer?" Superintendent Atwood Bland asked after greeting Washburn at his office door. "I've been simply devastated by the news of Roberta Dumond's death. She was such a stalwart supporter of that quaint and charming little church in her community," the superintendent continued.

"To the point, sir, is it true that a certain Clovis Netherdon has applied for the pastorship at that church?"

"Yes. But he was not recommended by the church board of trustees. And, under those circumstances, which we honor, we rejected his application."

"How did he feel about Mrs. Dumond?"

"Well, he exhibited some hostility toward her—blamed her for blackballing him."

"Was he here last Wednesday? Most of the day?"

"Yes, he was here, but certainly not most of the day."

"When, then? And for how long?"

"Let's see," the superintendent reflected for a few seconds, then reached into a drawer for his day-calendar. "To be exact, he had an appointment for 10:00 a.m. and was gone at 11:10. I know that for a fact because the pastor of a church in Albemarle County had an appointment for 11:15, and my secretary buzzed me to say he had arrived five minutes early. That's when Mr. Netherdon exited my office. I have not met with him since."

"What was the purpose of his appointment last Wednesday?"

"To ask for re-consideration, same as he had done in numerous phone calls. I denied his request."

"Thank you very much for your time, Superintendent Bland. I know you're a busy man."

"Well, of course. But I always have time for law enforcement trying to make a situation right. Is Mr. Netherdon guilty?"

"We don't know yet. He's being treated only as a person of interest at this time."

"I see. Well, then, my best wishes for good luck in your endeavors, officer."

On his way out of Charlottesville, Washburn suddenly detoured to the Albemarle County sheriff's office and asked to speak to an investigator. He made a very succinct request: Would the investigator and fellow deputies inquire of known prostitutes in and around town if Netherdon was a current client.

Back in Lovingston, he dropped by Town Mountain Realty. Blair was there, having spent several hours catching up on backlog work, now readying to leave for the day. She popped out of her office when she heard the front door slam shut on its spring hinge.

"Oh!" she exclaimed when she saw Washburn standing in the reception room, just inside the door.

"Am I intruding? Are you busy?" he asked, feigning shyness.

"Uh . . . no . . . not really. Actually I was readying to close shop. Come on in," she added, turning back to her office door.

"You sure? Don't want to detain you if you're in a hurry," he said apologetically, following her to the office.

"No, no. No hurry. I was just a bit startled to see you a minute ago. Here, have a seat," she directed, pointing to the chair in front of her desk.

He sat and crossed his legs, his posture and manner deliberately nonchalant. "Thought you might want to know the latest—again speaking against office policy, of course," he grinned conspiratorially.

"Of course!" she smiled back michievously.

Washburn spent a few minutes catching her up on activity occurring in the investigation after their phone conversation Sunday night.

"You agree with Sheriff Oakley? The case against Netherdon *is* getting tighter?" she asked when he finished his account.

"Seems like. If the hair from the Durango or the blood that was luminoled later in its cargo area came from Mr. Dumond or Lauren, the case should be cinched. Unless he has a credible alibi for last Wednesday afternoon."

"Yeah, credible is the magic word," Blair reflected, recalling what he had said was his request to the Albemarle deputies. "You've gotten blood and hair samples from Lauren already?"

"Sure."

"Of course you alredy had samples from Bert. When will you get the lab reports on tests?"

"Next Tuesday, I think. The twenty-second."

"What're you doing until then?"

"Going out with you. I hope," he answered, grinning shyly, left eyebrow lifted quizically.

"Whatever are you talking about?" she retorted playfully, coyily.

"A date."

"Ned, are you *serious*?"

"Yes. Absolutely."

Blair looked at his face, hearing the changed tone in his voice. He held her gaze, his eyes sparkling with anticipation, the grinning and teasing totally gone.

"But you can't be. You know the . . . the situation . . . my . . ." she trailed off, stumbling. Vulnerable now. Playfulness totally gone from *her* manner, too.

Both fell silent for a minute, the atmosphere overwhelmingly charged. Then Washburn got up quickly and moved to the corner of her desk. He sat on the desk's edge, dangling one leg, and clasped one of her hands.

"Yes, Blair, I know . . . your situation. And I understand. But I also know that I'm terribly attracted to you, that I care so much—"

"Oh, Ned . . . we can't—"

"Can't we? Blair, look at me," he invited softly. When she looked up at him, tears forming in her eyes, he continued, "You feel something, too. Don't you?"

"Yes, but—"

"Ssssh," he shushed soothingly as her eyes welled over, and, standing, gently pulled her up to stand closely in front of him.

They simply gazed into each other's eyes for seconds, perhaps looking for answers, perhaps just mesmerized. Then he put his arms around her and pulled her closer. She did not resist. He kissed her. She responded. Their lips parted, then locked again. And again, more passionately. Then Washburn kissed away the teardrops on her eyelids and cheeks. Blair pulled back enough to look at him, then tenderly traced his jawline with her fingertips.

"Ned, I need some time," she whispered against his cheek.

"I know," he whispered back.

They held each other for moments longer, before Washburn released her and stepped back a little.

"Look," he said, making an effort to rein in his emotions, to sound as matter-of-fact as he could. "I've got to be in Lexington Saturday. Will you drive over and have dinner with me?"

"How could I *possibly* arrange that? You know . . . with—"

"Just say you have a real estate appointment," he offered quickly. "Logical, isn't it?"

"Well . . . I guess so. It's just—"

"Blair," Washburn interrupted, touching fingers lightly to her forearm. "We'll *just* be having dinner. You won't be hurting anyone. And I know a restaurant . . . different . . . in an historic building. We can have drinks, a really good dinner, conversation. Be relaxing for you after the past week's horrors. Please say you will," he coaxed, hands now cupping her face.

"Well . . . all right. You've convinced me. What's the restaurant?" she asked, returning to a lighter mode herself.

"Wilson-Walker House. On Main Street. Six o'clock."

"Okay. I think I can find it. Now get out of here. Before I change my mind!"

"Okay!" Washburn echoed exclamatorily. He bussed her cheek, then left hastily.

Blair walked into the reception room and watched from a window to see Ned get into his car. "Oh boy! WHAT am I doing?" she asked aloud, in consternation. But she tingled with pleasure when she felt the lingering pressure of his arms on her ribcage as she crossed her arms over her chest—and moved her tongue over a puffy lower lip.

Landis and her friend Peter Mason flew into Dulles Airport Wednesday morning. Their cruise ship had docked in Florida the night before. They retrieved Landis's Mercedes convertible from the parking facility, the new Mercedes being the luxury to which Landis had treated herself following the previous year's open-house murder and subsequent bonanza of sales commissions. They took I-66 to Route 29, stopped in Charlottesville for lunch, then drove on to Peter's Afton home, where Landis dropped him off.

Back in the Lovingston area, Landis first paid a visit to Lauren—and got a colorful description of the week's events.

"Wow, did the mice ever play while this ole cat was away!" Landis said, laughing mockingly after hearing Lauren's account of Denny Olsey's three follow-up visits to her after he and his hunter friends found her.

"Mice? Hey, I'm only one mouse. Yuk, what an analogy for me to make!"

"Sorry. I keep forgetting your phobias."

"That's okay. But what did you mean by *mice*?"

"Blair. Think she may have something going, too."

"Blair? Like what?"

"Don't know yet. Exactly," Landis confessed. Then reconsidering, aware that she might have compromised Blair inadvertently, she added, "Might not be anything. Other than stress. But I must say, ya'll sure did have *drama* while I was gone!"

"THAT'S an understatement!"

"Well . . . look, you be sure to take it easy for awhile longer, okay. No need to hurry back to the office. I'm going by there when I leave here, to get messages and see if there's anything urgent to be taken care of. Do you know if Blair has been in?"

"Yes. Monday. And yesterday, too, for awhile. I don't know about today."

"She told me about spraining an ankle. How's she doing now?" Landis asked.

"Getting along pretty well, I think. I know she's dropped the crutch."

"Good. I'll call her in a bit. She invited me to dinner tonight. Hope it's still on. Talk to you later, gal."

On those parting words Landis dashed out the door. Leaving Lauren to speculate about her reference to Blair's having "something going". No doubt shrewd and canny Lauren would have the mystery solved quickly. After all, she knew these two women *very* well.

FOURTEEN

Dinner at Blair Camfield's meant a well-prepared meal and catch-up conversation but not an occasion for private talk. The children, Whitley and Meade, particularly wanted to hear descriptions of the enchanting places Landis's cruise had included and details of activities in which Landis and Peter had participated. Richard was interested mostly in a fishing side-trip they had taken. Blair, for her part, elicited information about the ship's accommodations and interesting people aboard.

Thursday was devoted to Roberta Dumond's funeral service, followed by a reception at the Dumond home. Blair, Landis, Lauren, and Ned Washburn were among the attendees.

It was not until Friday that Landis had an opportunity to remind Blair of her promise to reveal what was bothering her, apparently even causing some depression. Barely through the real estate office back door into the kitchen Friday morning, Landis confronted Blair, who was standing at the coffee maker.

"Okay, pal, it's high time to talk."

"Well, *pal*, you think maybe I could have a cup of coffee first!" Blair retorted jokingly.

"Sure. Pour one for me, too," Landis returned, just as tires on gravel announced the arrival of Lauren. She knew it was Lauren because a customer wouldn't be driving right up to the back door.

"Put it in styrofoam cups. Quick!" Landis commanded as she heard a car door slamming shut. Blair cast a puzzled look at Landis but said nothing as she poured the coffee.

"Well, how about this? All three of us together again! Like old times," Lauren greeted them exuberantly as she entered the kitchen.

"Damn lucky to be, too!" Landis exclaimed to underscore the sentiment. "But are you sure you feel ready to get back to work so soon?" she added.

"Sure do. Been homebound longer than enough. Besides, the doc says I'm good to go."

"Okay, great. Especially considering that Blair and I have an appointment. Be gone a couple hours or so," Landis said, giving Blair a look which conveyed the message for Blair not to contradict her.

Nevertheless, Lauren sensed a conspiratorial undercurrent and did not ask her proverbial question: "Where're you going?"

"See you when you get back," she said instead, and turned to the coffee pot to pour herself a cup.

Continuing the charade of a business appointment, Landis elected to drive the company stationwagon. Neither she nor Blair said anything until they had left the office lot and travelled south on Route 29 for nearly five miles. When they turned west on Tye Brook Highway, Landis opened conversation with a question about the status of a sales contract she had negotiated a week before leaving on the cruise. They turned right on Roseland Road and continued chatting about aspects of pending business transactions.

When Landis made a left turn on Route 151 and travelled no more than two hundred feet before making a sharp right turn onto Route 56 West, Blair knew exactly where they were going. To Crabtree Falls, one of Landis's favorite spots in the county—especially when she wanted privacy in a serene, though public, place.

At the parking lot near the footbridge over the south fork of Tye River, Landis drove to a slot fartherest from the bridge. There were only two other cars in the lot. Both were parked at the front, very close to the bridge footpath. Both were empty, their passengers off on a climb up the falls.

"I've already figured what's bothering you, Blair. It's Ned Washburn," Landis said flatly, off-setting a denial.

"Why do you say that?" Blair returned, mildly defensive, mostly stalling for time.

"Because I've got eyes—and instincts! I didn't miss the charged atmosphere surrounding you two yesterday afternoon at Roberta's house either. Now, tell me, just exactly what's going on?"

"Nothing's *going on*, Lan—"

"Well, then, *getting ready to go on*! I'm not a fool, Blair. I recognize the signs."

"He's attracted to me. I mean . . ."

"Hell, I can see that! But what about *you*?"

"I . . . well . . . it's not that simple."

"Very little in life is, Blair. But again, I ask: ARE YOU ATTRACTED TO HIM? Even falling for him?" Landis challenged.

"Yes, dammit!" Blair snapped. "There! Now you have it." She stopped talking, looked down at her clasped hands in her lap. "I don't know how it happened, Lan. I surely wasn't looking for anything like this," she resumed softly.

"But apparently you were ripe and ready!"

"LANDIS! The last thing I need is your sarcasm. Look . . . Oh, let's just drop the subject."

"No, no, let's not. We can't."

"Why not?" Blair challenged.

"Because you're my friend, Blair. You're conflicted, no doubt hurting, and probably heading for big trouble. I need to help you understand the situation."

"Landis, I *understand the situation*! As you put it," Blair countered, apparently forgetting that it was she who had referred to her "situation" when she was talking to Ned Washburn. "It's my *feelings* I don't understand."

"Well, that's what I meant. Look, I'm sorry for the remark, and I apologize for the way I blundered into this conversation. Let me try again, start over. Okay?"

"Okay," Blair responded weakly.

"Blair, I love you. You're my best friend. When you hurt, I hurt for you. I may not know your every aspect, but I know a lot about you. I know that you love your family; that you're loyal and responsible; that you're kind and caring; that you're spiritual, have a strong faith and moral compass—"

"Ha! Moral compass! That from *you*, Lan?" Blair charged.

"Yes, that from me. I have a moral compass, too. Of sorts. It's just different from yours," Landis qualified.

"So if *you* have an extra-marital relationship, it's fine and dandy, huh?"

"Now who's being sarcastic? First of all, Blair, remember *I'm* not married, so I can't have extra-marital affairs, fine and dandy or not. Second, by moral compass I mean only that I have a code."

"Care to define it, describe it?"

"Be glad to. It's simply a philosophy I settled on for myself a long time ago: Be truthful, be kind, be more giving than expecting, be rational rather than emotional in thought and action, be joyful rather than depressive, be loving and—"

"Whew! Care to relate all that to a relationship?" Blair interrupted.

"I was trying to. The rest was, be loving and *faithful.* Fifty-fifty. I give what I expect in return. Anything less, a relationship is dead."

"And your marriage to Michael wasn't fifty-fifty?"

"In all ways except two: constant togetherness and children. He wanted both. I didn't."

"What about Peter?"

"We have a good balance."

"Are you going to get married?"

"No."

"Why not? I don't understand. You're talking in circles, Lan. Don't you love him?"

"Yes, I do. Adore him, in fact."

"Then why not get married?"

"Love . . . adoration . . . and marriage are not necessarily synonymous."

"Landis! Plain speak, please."

"Okay. I love Peter. He loves me. We share common attitudes, points of view, and interests. You know—sports, the theatre, reading, travelling—the whole nine yards. We're playmates, friends, companions, lovers. What we're not—and don't want to be—are twenty-four-sevens."

"What, pray tell, is *that*?"

"We don't want to be together twenty-four hours a day, seven days a week. We like some apartness, some 'his and hers'—you know, separate activity. No matter how much I love Peter, or someone else, I don't want to *live* with anybody *all* the time!"

"Don't you get lonely sometimes?"

"I have absolutely no idea what loneliness is, Blair. I love living, doing, staying involved. I'm with people when I want to be, and I'm comfortable with myself when I'm alone. I don't believe that one's happiness or contentment should be dependent upon another person's provision. It has to be a personal achievement."

"I must admit you do seem comfortable in your own skin. But Lan, surely one *can* have a separate identity in a marriage?"

"Identity, yes, of course. But not independence, I think."

"I have independence."

"Do you? Think about it, Blair. Do you go where you want, do what you want, see whom you want—when you want?"

"I don't have to ask permission, if that's what you mean."

"No, it's not. I mean you have to be accountable, be available for others' needs. Perhaps even have to explain or justify any deviation in your routine sometimes."

"Touché," Blair said, laughing. "Enough said. Of course, I *accept* that as an integral part of my lifestyle."

"I know you do. And that's commendable. For you. We simply have different philosophies. No problem."

"Frankly, however, I've secretly admired your lifestyle from time to time. Which brings me back to where we started this conversation. To Ned Washburn. Maybe some of the attraction for me is his self-sufficiency, authoritativeness. So unlike Richard's neediness and dependency upon me for decision-making."

"Good move. Let's do get back to the purpose of this talk while we have time," Landis readily agreed, inwardly sighing, glad to get the subject off herself finally. "What do you plan to do about Ned?"

"I don't know . . . not sure."

"What is he proposing? Your divorcing? Or just having an affair?"

"He's not proposing anything. Well, not other than dinner in Lexington Saturday."

"Oh, I thought . . . I mean, on the phone you sounded so upset—"

"Things haven't moved *that* fast, Lan—though pretty fast, considering it's been only ten days! As I said, it's my feelings that have me confused. Actually *astounded* is more like it. I've never before felt such a *pull* toward anyone—really, as if it's outside me, as if I have no control over it. What do you think?"

"I think it's because you and Ned came together under stressful circumstances, at a time when you were alone and vulnerable. You found Ned strong, supportive, compassionate, providing the romance lacking in Richard's unexpressive, old-shoe personality. Feelings got mixed, melded—"

"That's true, Lan, but it's more, too," Blair interjected.

"And that's why you have to decide what you're going to do about it. Pretty soon."

"I know. I thought I *had* decided. Twice. To tell him the next time I saw him that we had to nix the feelings, that nothing could develop between us. Then when I saw him, the decision just went by the wayside. What do you think I should do? *That's* what I've been wanting to ask *you*! Since the minute I first felt attracted to him."

"I shouldn't tell you what to do, Blair."

"But you'd like to! So, go ahead. Be my guest."

"Okay. Since you put it that way, here it is: If you can play and not hurt anyone in the process, not get burned yourself—if indeed you can handle a double-life, then GO for it. If you can't, then cut and run now. Personally, I don't think you can handle an affair, be unfaithful. That's what I was trying to get at back there when we veered off on a big limb. Uk-uh, wait, hold it!" Landis cautioned when Blair attempted to interrupt. "I'm not finished. I was going to say, however, that you need to realize, too, that what you're feeling is not real love, not what will sustain you for the long haul."

"What are you getting at?"

"While Ned Washburn is handsome, intelligent, witty—an all-round attractive guy, even an exciting guy—his lifestyle is not compatible with your needs. He's an intense workaholic, Blair, not a family man, and certainly not a long-term playmate. That's what ended his marriage."

"How do *you* know that?"

"He told me. You probably didn't realize that he and I got to be fairly good buddies after that murder case last year."

"You mean, you two . . ." Blair intoned, eyebrows flying high.

"No, Blair, no personal involvement. He and his wife were having problems last fall, about to divorce, and for some reason he sought me out. He needed someone to listen, maybe advise. I played devil's advocate. That's all. Besides, remember, I had just met Peter Mason, and had the hots for *him*!"

Blair laughed loudly, in spite of the moment, remembering Landis's near-swoon when she first saw Peter enter a room. "So you know Ned pretty well, huh?"

"Enough."

"Meaning you don't like him?"

"Quite the contrary. I like him very much. In fact, I think he and I would make a helluva team. Detective partners, you know!" Landis bragged airily.

They sat in silence for some seconds, both caught up in private thoughts, worn down by the emotional exchanges.

"Hey, guess we'd better get back to the office," Landis said, breaking the silence, and proceeded to start the stationwagon. As they were nearing Silver Creek Packing Shed at Tyro, Landis re-approached the subject. "Blair, you do what you must or what you think is best concerning Ned. Just keep in mind the interests and feelings of Whitley, Meade, and Richard. I'm not going to lecture you again, or criticize. Whatever you do, I'll support you. And I'll be available and open-minded anytime you want to talk. Okay, pal?"

"Okay, pal! And thanks. I mean it."

Landis drove onto the shoulder of the road, west of Massies Mill, and stopped.

"Shake?" she asked.

They shook hands, smiling at each other affectionately but a little self-consciously following so much personal revelation. Then Blair scooted closer to Landis, and the two friends hugged—in front of God and the staring passengers in two passing cars!

FIFTEEN

Following a late lunch at Vito's Friday, Blair, Landis, and Lauren retreated to the real estate office.

"Where's the anti-acid?" Landis called from one of the restrooms. "I thought we kept it in the cabinet in here."

"It's on the kitchen sink, Landis," Lauren called back. "Right where you left it last time."

"Well, if it weren't for your *fan* club I wouldn't need it!" Landis retorted, stomping off to the kitchen.

"Who *were* all those people, Lauren?" Blair followed up. "I could hardly take a bite between onslaughts! It's not surprising Landis got indigestion."

"Gosh, I didn't know all of them myself! Members of various clubs I work with, church acquaintances, parents of my children's friends, etc., I guess. Just curious to see how I'd fared in my 'adventure', as you put it."

"I knew you were popular, but, boy, looks like you know half the county!"

"Ya'll ought to be glad I do. Helps business!"

"You're right, it does. And we *are* glad," Landis offered, walking back into the reception room from the kitchen. "Now, get busy and make some money! Me, I don't feel like working. Think I'll call Washburn and ask him to come over. Maybe he can use my help on this case."

Lauren rolled her eyes in mock dismay. "Oh yeah, no doubt!" she sneered.

Blair had turned and walked to her office at mention of Washburn's name.

Lauren noticed. "What's with her?" she whispered to Landis.

"Can't say anything now. She'll tell you later, I'm sure," Landis whispered back. "You got any appointments this afternoon?" she asked in a loud voice to off-set the silence for Blair's benefit.

"No appointments, but a lot of calls to make."

"See you later, then," Landis said, and proceeded to walk to her own office.

When Washburn arrived thirty minutes later, Lauren directed him to Landis's office. She didn't miss his momentary hesitation at Blair's open door. "Ha, don't think I'll have to wait to be told!" she mumbled, inaudibly.

"Hey, fella, long time no see," Landis greeted Washburn from behind her desk, then stood to shake hands.

"You're looking great! Heard you were away on a cruise," Washburn commented. "Accounts for such a good tan in late October, huh?"

"Sure does. But I was ready to get back here to my mountains and valleys. Nothing like it in this part of America, Ned!"

"I kinda like it around here myself," Ned agreed.

"So I gather," Landis returned, tongue-in-cheek.

"Meaning?"

"Nothing really."

"Has Blair said something?"

"Didn't have to. She's my friend . . . I know her well. Look, just take it easy, buddy, hear me?"

"Landis, I—"

"Don't go there, Ned," Landis cut him off. "Enough said. For now. Let's get to business. How's the case going?"

"You know I can't divulge details."

"Huumph!" Landis snorted. "So, generalize."

"Blair's probably told you that we consider Clovis Netherdon a person of interest," Washburn offered.

"Ah, come on, Ned. Sounds to me more like you have a pretty good case against him," Landis wheedled.

"One thing that does puzzle me is a broken parking light lens found by a hunter on one of those backroads—logging trails, or whatever they are. Bob Herman researched the lens on the Internet and learned it's from a Dodge Durango. We checked out five Durangos, including Netherdon's, but none of them had a broken lens."

"Huumm," Landis reflected. "How old is his Durango?"

"Three years."

"And his was the only Durango with tire treads that matched what ya'll photographed, right?"

"Uh . . . right," Washburn responded, squirming a little. Obviously Blair had shared more than he liked.

"Well, then, that gives *me* something to work on," Landis said smugly.

"Hey, now, not so fast, *buddy*! You can't just go off on one of your 'sleuthing' tangents in *this* investigation. I'd be lucky if you didn't get me fired," Washburn protested.

"No way! Don't worry. I have no intention of getting into your business. But I have an idea, see. Means I'd be operating on the sidelines."

"Hell, I probably can't stop you anyway, so I'll just save my breath. But, please, Landis, for heaven's sake, don't mess with anybody—"

"You sure as hell don't have to worry about *that*! This old gal got a bellyful of *confrontation* last year!" Landis asserted vehemently.

"All right, then, I have your word, right? No interference with the official investigation, no impersonating law enforcement personnel—"

"You got it! No trouble from me," she promised, overriding what else he might have said.

They parted with "See you later's". Back in the reception room, Washburn detoured to Blair's office.

"Hey," he called softly from her open doorway.

Blair looked up—and smiled a response.

For Lauren's benefit, he spoke louder. "How's the ankle?"

"Almost good as new," Blair responded in normal volume.

"Great. Take care. See you later," he continued in normal volume also, then mouthed for Blair's eyes only, "Tomorrow, six."

Blair nodded. "See you," she echoed.

Washburn made a point to linger at Lauren's desk in the reception room near the front door.

"When did you get back to work?"

"Today," Lauren answered bluntly.

"Feeling okay?"

"Pretty much. Still a little sluggiesh, but getting stronger every day."

"Good. We should get the lab reports the middle of next week. I'll be in touch," Washburn promised.

"Thanks, I—"

Lauren was interrupted by the phone ringing. She answered in her throaty but professional voice, then immediately said, "Just a moment, please." She hit the Hold button. "Excuse me, I need to take this call," she said to Washburn.

As he wiggled fingers in farewell, smiled, and opened the door, she turned back to the phone. When the door snapped shut, she said, "Hi, Denny," in sugary voice.

Washburn was leaving the reception room when Landis pulled the Lynchburg and Charlottesville phone directories off her book shelves. She flipped to the yellow pages in each and looked up Automobile Dealers. On a legal pad she wrote the numbers for John P. Hughes Dodge in Madison Heights and Brown's Dodge in Charlottesville.

First Landis phoned John P. Hughes Dodge and asked to speak to the body shop service manager. She told him that she was checking out the possibility that one of her children had brought her Durango there for a parking light lens replacement on October 9th, 10th, or 11th. He asked her name; she said, "Mrs. Netherdon." He ran a computer check on invoices for the dates she had named, and reported there was no such repair or replacement. She thanked him and asked to be transferred to the Parts Department. Same negative result: there had been no counter sale of a lens on those days.

Landis repeated the requests to Brown's Dodge in Charlottesville and got the same answers there. Then she sat silently for several minutes, hands steepled under her chin, contemplating. There *had* to be an answer to the riddle somewhere.

"Ah, ha!" she blurted after several minutes, and reached for the Richmond Yellow Pages. "Why didn't I think of this sooner? Richmond's only eighty-some miles from the Howardsville area, and I bet lots of people down there go to Richmond all the time," she continued, still talking to herself as she looked up Dodge dealers.

Landis jotted down the number and location of four dealers, alphabetically: Chesterfield Dodge, Mechanicsville Dodge, Pence Chrysler/Plymouth/ Dodge/Jeep, and West End Dodge. She repeated the ploy: that one of her children had sneaked her Durango off somewhere for repair to avoid her detection and she was trying to pin it down. And struck gold on the fourth call!

At West End Dodge body shop she was told, yes, a three-year-old Durango had been serviced on October 10; indeed, a lens was replaced, Invoice #0402196.

"What name's on the invoice?" Landis asked breathlessly, left-hand fingers crossed. She quickly jotted down the invoice number.

"None. Sorry. On cash payments for minor repairs we don't usually ask a name. Didn't this time."

"Color?"

"No. Not filled in."

Landis thanked him and hung up abruptly. "Shoot! Thought for a second I really had something there!" she scoffed. And tossed the phone books to the floor, her adrenaline rush depleted.

Blair found late Saturday afternoon in Lexington to be simply gorgeous. Trees blazed with an eastern fall's brilliant colors under a harvest blue sky, lightly scattered leaves fluttered on old brick sidewalks, and a chill in the air invigorated smartly-dressed strollers to laugh and talk animatedly. Blair was enchanted. Although she had been to Lexington only several times, she loved the charming Colonial aspects of the town, reminiscent of similar streets in the older sections of Fredericksburg and Williamsburg. Blair, who lived in and loved a 1700's home herself, often felt that she belonged to an earlier century.

Ned Washburn was waiting for her in the foyer of Wilson-Walker House. He had made a reservation earlier in the week, requesting a table in the corner of a high-ceilinged front room near a fireplace. The room was dimly lighted, fire glowing. Tables were adorned with crisp cloths, fresh flower arrangements, and real candles. One had the sensation of dining in a stately private home.

No sooner had the hostess escorted them to their table than a wine-steward appeared at Washburn's elbow, with chilled napkin-wrapped wine bottle in the crook of his arm and ice bucket in his hand. Ned directed him to present to Blair for tasting. She sipped and smilingly nodded her approval. Actually she had found the taste toe-curlingly delightful. The steward proceeded to pour for them, then deposited the bottle in ice and departed. Washburn and Blair clinked glasses, toasting, as Ned put it, "a special evening".

They chatted about such things as the restaurant's charm, their impressions of the town, and the challenging drive over the mountain as they sipped wine and tried to ease into being together. Alone, apart from business, in an intimate setting.

In a few minutes a waiter interrupted to take their orders, after which a couple at the next table asked where they were from to open general conversation, which lasted fifteen minutes—thus breaking the ice and promoting comfort. Subsequent conversation between Washburn and Blair revealed a number of common interests, including fishing, gardening, reading, musical theatre, and antique furniture. They found that they also shared similar observations and impressions of personalities and "goings-on" in the Lovingston business and county-government world—and they laughed heartily as they exchanged anecdotes.

At nine o'clock Blair sipped the last of her second coffee and said, "This evening has been absolutely delightful, and I hate to end it, but I really must go. You know . . . an hour and a half for me to get home . . . longer if there's fog on the mountain."

Washburn walked her to her car. "Thanks for coming over. It was a lovely and fun evening for me," he said as he opened her door.

"It was for me, too, Ned. And dinner was divine! Thank you," she returned as she slipped behind the steering wheel.

Washburn leaned down and kissed her lightly. "Talk to you next week. Drive carefully," he added, and shut the driver's door.

Blair took the longer route back, by way of I-64 from Lexington to the Afton exit, thinking it safer and less deserted than the narrow, winding road from Vesuvius through Montebello and Massies Mill. Thus, with less concentration on road conditions, she was able to relive the dinner-date in her mind. She smiled her pleasure. It *had* been a lovely evening—indeed, the most romantic evening she had had since her first date with Richard. "And innocent, too," she declared. "Well, almost," she qualified, acknowledging her vaguely worded fib to Richard about the Lexington trip being work-related.

"Innocent for now," a little voice of conscience whispered.

SIXTEEN

Blair and Landis heard of no new developments in the investigation on Sunday or Monday. However, Blair was bombarded with questions at a memorial luncheon Sunday in honor of Roberta Dumond in the church's social hall following the regular service. Most were people who didn't attend church services there frequently, had not heard much about Roberta Dumond's murder, and were hungry for details from someone close to the scene.

At the realty office Monday Lauren got a call from Malcolm Earndahl, the man to whom she had shown the Bannister listing minutes before her kidnapping. He wanted to know how she was doing a week after her awful experience, he said, and also wanted to make an appointment to return to look at other properties.

"Now, wasn't that sweet?" Lauren posed rhetorically to Blair as soon as she hung up and described his call. "How did he know about me being rescued? Did you call him?"

"No. Ned did. He also called the Fairfax police to describe what actually happened to you, so as to clear away any question about Mr. Earndahl for them," Blair explained, still standing beside Lauren's desk.

"That was good of him. I'll try to remember to say thanks when I see him next. By the way, when are *you* seeing him again?"

"Me? When something new comes up in the case, I guess. Why?" Blair responded diffidently. She hoped her tone had sounded matter-of-fact, not revealing how startled she had been by Lauren's question.

The hope was immediately dashed. "I meant, when is your next date?" Lauren asked archly.

Blair's face turned ashen, then rosy as blood flooded back. "Did . . . did Landis say something—"

"Nope. Not a word!" Lauren cut in emphatically.

"Then who . . . I mean, what are you . . . how did you know?" Blair blundered.

"Blair, dear, I wasn't born yesterday. I can read signs. Especially when I know someone as well as I know you."

"When . . . what signs?"

"Body language. When you and Washburn are together. I first noticed something at the reception after Mrs. Dumond's funeral. Then last week here when Landis asked him to come over to meet with her. Neither you nor Washburn is a good actor, believe me! I'm telling you, if *you* don't want your feelings to show, you'd better take an acting lesson from Miss Oscar-winning Landis! And quick! Besides, I can read lips," Lauren added saucily.

"Read lips? For what?"

"Does 'Tomorrow, six' ring a bell?"

Again Blair's face blanched. She dropped into the "customer" chair beside Lauren's desk.

"I don't know what to say, Lauren," Blair said resignedly.

"You don't need to say a thing, Blair. Stuff happens. I'm not naive. And I'm not judgmental. Lord knows, I've had more than my share of emotional entanglements! Your personal business stays right here . . . you don't have to worry about my saying anything to anybody. But I will advise you to be careful. This *is* a small community, you know," Lauren cautioned. "Also I'd hate to see you get hurt," she added, gently patting Blair's arm where it rested on the desk's edge.

"Or my family. I know. Thanks, Lauren. For your understanding . . . for everything."

"How serious is it? Rather, how serious are you?"

"I don't know. About 'it' or me. That's just it—the confusing thing. I wasn't looking for, nor expecting, an involvement . . . a relationship. And so far it's not one. But I don't know if I'll *stop* one developing."

"I expect you'll know what to do when the time comes."

"Why do you say that?"

"Oh, I think old common sense rides to the rescue when needed. Or maybe more accurately it's a woman's intuition that directs her decision to go one way or the other. For her, the best way."

"You mean her understanding of the other person will tell her whether or not to gamble on an involvement?"

"Or her understanding of herself."

Silence fell between the two women for long moments. Then just as Blair opened her mouth to say something, the back door burst open and Landis popped in energetically.

"Hey, gals, you'll never guess what I just sold that old dilapidated property on Horseshoe Road for. You know, the one I bought last year," Landis bragged.

"No. But tell us quickly before we die from bated breath!" Lauren retorted.

"Huh? What's going on here?" Landis asked, belatedly realizing that she had interrupted something.

"She figured it out," Blair murmurred, bending a thumb in Lauren's direction.

"Figured what out?"

"Ned and me."

"Well, hot damn! Next thing we know she'll have a 'Dear Lauren' column in the Nelson County Times!"

"Landis!" Blair reprimanded.

"Hey, I meant it as a compliment. We've always known Lauren is keen—a really sharp cookie indeed. You shouldn't have been surprised. But you should be considering how many other sharp cookies are out there!"

"Just what I cautioned," Lauren echoed.

"Okay, okay. Enough. I get the point," Blair conceded, getting up and walking toward her office. At her door she turned around. "But thanks. To both of you," she said, smiling, then disappeared into her office and shut the door. Not her usual habit.

Landis and Lauren exchanged glances. And shrugged simultaneously.

"Well, guess I'd better get to work, too," Landis announced, proceeding to her office.

"Hold it!" Lauren called. "What were you going to say about your sale?"

"Oh, nothing much. Just netted $50,000 profit, that's all," Landis tossed back flippantly.

On Tuesday, October 22 the sheriff's office received the lab report on tests of the evidence found in Clovis Netherdon's Durango the previous week. Washburn visited Town Mountain Realty at 11:00. Landis, Blair, and Lauren were all there. As was a county resident who had dropped in to discuss listing his property with them. Washburn chatted idly with Lauren at the kitchen table until the other two concluded their business with the drop-in, setting up an appointment to visit his property to do an informal appraisal the following week.

"Hey, bud, what's up?" Landis called as she and Blair entered the kitchen. She slapped Washburn's back in further greeting as she moved past him to sit at the head of the table. Lauren got up to fetch coffee for everyone.

"Got some news. Still in confidence, okay?" he began, and waited for them to acknowledge agreement before continuing. "Lab report we received this morning confirms that Netherdon's SUV *was* used in both crimes. Hair found in it belonged to Roberta Dumond. Blood . . . well, that was yours, Lauren."

"Wow!" Landis blurted. "That's it, then. He's the perp!"

"Not so fast there," Washburn cautioned. "I'm not sure of that. Not yet."

"Why not?" Blair asked. "His vehicle—"

"Oh, of course his vehicle is involved," Washburn injected. "That, plus the tire iron from the Durango that hunters found Sunday, means we have enough for probable cause. Enough to arrest him." He stopped and looked at his watch. "In fact, right about now Deputies Taskell and Douglas are taking him into custody."

"Tire iron? Denny didn't say anything. Where was it found?" Lauren asked, her interest clearly piqued.

"Denny wasn't along. They found it in a shallow draw not far from the shack where you were found. It was in a Food Lion plastic bag, tangled in honeysuckle vines. Some of the hunters who went there to clean the shack for use during deer season caught sight of the bag when wind ruffled it. Simple curiosity prompted them to check it out," Washburn elaborated.

"You think that's the weapon used to hit me?" Lauren asked, instinctively touching fingers to the back of her head.

"Very possibly. No doubt probably. We sent it to the lab yesterday to be checked for prints, tissue, hair, blood. Fortunately, the hunters didn't touch it, just looked in the bag."

"So what happens now?" Blair asked.

"Well, Netherdon will be brought in, processed and incarcerated at the regional jail, then arraigned on the next scheduled court day. But we have a lot of work to do still. The investigation is very much on-going."

"To find what, for instance?" Landis asked.

"Mainly verification for the time-line of Netherdon's movements on October 9. Albemarle deputies are working on that for us. And the mystery of that darn lens is still hanging in the air, too. We checked repair shops all over cental Virginia and had no luck. Now we're checking junkyard businesses to see if any inquiries were made for a used lens on October 9 or 10. If that effort doesn't pan out, I guess we'll have to solicit information regarding a lens stolen from someone's vehicle," Washburn summarized.

Landis said nothing about her calls to Dodge dealers. No point risking antagonizing Washburn. Apparently he hadn't heard about her inquiries. Besides, she had learned nothing.

"Anything we can do to help?" Lauren asked.

"Not right now, thanks. Unless you can remember something about your kidnapping, of course! Meanwhile, Blair, do you and Landis have anything to report?" Washburn asked slyly.

Both said no. He smiled broadly, pushed his chair back from the table, and stood. "You know, I heard a funny thing yesterday. Seems a fella in the parts department at Brown's Dodge in Charlottesville remembered that *Mrs. Netherdon* had called to find out if one of her children had bought a parking light lens for her vehicle. Interesting development, don't you think?"

Blair and Lauren looked at each other quizically. Landis steepled her hands beneath her chin and stared at the wall, brows puckered as if reflecting deep concentration.

Washburn signaled Blair and Lauren to look at Landis. His point silently made, their laughter then blended with his in enjoyment of Landis's discomfort. They were still smiling when he turned back at the door and said before exiting, "I'll keep ya'll posted on developments. But, remember, mum's the word. See you later."

Clovis Netherdon was arraigned Thursday. He pled "Not Guilty". Commonwealth Attorney Paul Parker argued against bail, saying that Netherdon was a flight risk because he had no family or commitments in the county and was charged with two felonies: a murder and a kidnapping. Despite Charlottesville defense attorney Terry Bagley's pleas for a reasonable bail bond, the district court judge ruled that Netherdon be remanded. Deputies cuffed him and returned him to the regional jail.

The preliminary hearing was scheduled on the court's calendar for November 5.

At the commonwealth attorney's request, Washburn, Della Dumond Shales, and Lauren met with him at his office the next morning, Friday. Their depositions began the formal case against Clovis Netherdon.

SEVENTEEN

"*Never*? Really, you've never flown?" Ned Washburn asked, in the same incredulous tone people always use when they encounter someone who hasn't experienced, or probably mastered, *all* modern technology, especially that pertaining to computers, telecommunications, and music recordation. The recipients of such intonations always interpret them to be condescending.

"I didn't say I had never flown. I said I don't fly. Meaning, I don't particularly like flying," Blair countered.

"When was the last time?"

"Uh . . . twelve years ago . . . no, thirteen, I think."

"A commercial flight?"

"No. A helicopter."

"Well, heavens, Blair, that doesn't begin to compare to flying in a Cessna four-seater! Come on, say you'll go. Please. It'll be fun," Washburn pleaded and promised.

"I don't know . . . You say it's your plane?"

"One-third mine. Two friends share ownership. Works out great. We use it at different times, anyway, and sharing expenses lessens the burden for each of us."

"Where do you keep it?"

"At Waynesboro Airport."

"And how long have you been flying?" she grilled.

"One year in this plane. Ten years total experience. No accidents, no problems."

"Well, I'll think about it," Blair conceded reluctantly. She didn't exactly chicken-out when it came to adventure. After all, she loved the speed of fast cars, boats, skiing, and snowboarding. But flying? She supposed she just felt a lot less in control.

It was late afternoon on Saturday. Washburn and Blair were driving to Waynesboro in his car. She had met him at The Country Store, located at the intersection of Routes 6 and 250, and left her car parked there. His invitation had been for dinner at Captain Sam's. Now he was proposing taking her on a short flight in his plane before dinner.

"Okay. You have a five-mile deadline for a decision," Washburn quipped, and reached for her hand.

They entered I-64 at the top of Afton Mountain and descended to the Shenandoah Valley. Blair rode in silence until they were in sight of the main Waynesboro exit.

"Okay, I'll try it," she said, breaking the silence.

"Try it? I'm afraid, my dear, that it's fly or not fly. There's no *try to fly*," Washburn returned, chuckling.

"I mean I'll get in the plane, see how it *feels*, and then decide to go up or not," she explained. "Fair enough?"

"Fair enough. Besides, if you don't trust me to take it up on my own, I can ask an instructor to go along as co-pilot. Of course, I would prefer to have *you* sit up front. Much better experience for you."

At the airport Blair saw only private aircraft. Obviously it was not a major commercial terminal. She climbed to the co-pilot's seat of the Cessna 210, with some assistance from Washburn, thinking all the while how fortunate she was to have worn slacks. She sat there while Washburn completed his checklist, at first just observing the bustling activities of staff and owners going back and forth from terminal building to aircraft, then transferring her attention to studying the instrument panel. The feel of the cabin was not unlike that of a sports car, it seemed to her. "Maybe this won't be *so* bad," she muttered, consoling herself and bracing for the ride.

Blair's reservations had been for naught. She found the fast acceleration down the runway and the power of lift-off to be exciting—invigorating even. But those experiences paled in comparison to the thrill she felt in her every fiber when, at Washburn's direction, she took the co-pilot's yoke in her hands and he removed his from the pilot's yoke, leaving her in full control. For the few minutes that she piloted the plane, banking right then left and getting a feather-light response from the plane in return, she knew that for the first and last time in her life she had felt the specialness, the near-spirituality, of soaring in space. When Washburn resumed piloting, she just sat back trance-like, savoring the sensation.

At Captain Sam's later, during several scrumptious seafood courses, embellished by an excellent bottle of white zinfandel, Blair couldn't stop chattering about her flying experience.

Pleased and flattered, Washburn reached across the table and squeezed her hand. "I promised it would be fun, didn't I?" he beamed.

"That you did! I shouldn't have doubted you."

"I have another idea—proposal—that could be fun, too," he offered coyly.

"Oh? Like what?" she quipped.

In response he placed a key on the table, a key attached to a ring that also contained a piece of black plastic displaying the number 509. A motel key.

Blair stared at it, all her light-heartedness squashed. "Damn," she thought, "a sweet evening jolted to an end."

After silent moments, Blair looked up at Washburn, straight into his eyes. "Ned," she said softly, unshed tears softening her own eyes, "I like you. A lot. I really do." She placed a hand on his wrist. "You're a great date, great fun to be with, a very interesting person. But I'm not ready for that," she asserted gently, pointing to the key. "Not yet," she added before she could bite off the qualifying words. "Do you understand?"

"I think so," he said, and patted her hand. "I didn't mean to offend you."

"You didn't. And I hope you don't think I've mis-led you."

"I don't."

"Then let's change the topic—and order some dessert!"

"Hey, Richard, how're you doing?" Landis greeted Richard Camfield when his secretary showed her into his office Monday afternoon.

"Fine. How're you, Landis?"

"I'm good. Tax work keeping you busy these days?" she chattered away.

"Steady. Nothing like January through August, though. What can I do for you? Joan didn't say you gave a reason for making this appointment."

"Well, tell the truth, Rich, I'm not here on business. Least, not today. It's kinda personal," Landis rambled vaguely. Rather uncharacteristic for her.

"Oh? In that case, Landis, I ought to tell you right off that it's not likely I'll be able to help you," Richard said, plainly awkward and embarrassed.

"Not personal about *me*, Rich! Look, I'm sorry to make this more awkward than it was gonna be anyway. Let me start over, come right to the point. I'm here to talk about Blair—and you, sort of."

"Blair? Is something wrong concerning Blair?" the man almost shouted, bolting upright from his chair, clearly distraught by the possibility that Blair might be hurt, ready to run from his office.

"No, Richard. Sit down! Nothing's wrong. Well, not yet anyway. It's just that . . . well, Blair needs more attention."

"More attention? I don't understand."

"That's what I figured." Landis simply couldn't resist the double-entendre. "Richard, you and Blair have been married for . . . what? . . . twelve years or so?"

"Yes. Twelve and a few months."

"Well, with the children to care for and the two businesses and the farm and community activities and all kinds of stuff taking up a lot of time and energy, you and Blair don't have much quality time for just yourselves any longer. Together, I mean."

"You think then that maybe she's feeling neglected?" Richard asked.

Hot dog, Landis thought, he's getting the point!

Then he added, "I know I've felt a little that way lately."

Oh, great! "See, Richard, you do understand," Landis waded on. "Both of you need a shot of . . . of . . . well, romance. You need to do little special things for each other, plan surprises, stuff like that. And go on a date once a week. Shoot, I'll even keep the children while you're out!"

Richard continued to look at Landis after she stopped talking, long enough for her to wonder if she'd pushed too hard, gone too far. Then suddenly, beaming an ear-to-ear smile, he reached across his desk and shook her hand.

"Great idea, Landis! Thanks. Wish I'd thought of it myself."

"I wish you had, too," she mumbled inwardly, and stood. "Deal, then?" she asked.

"Absolutely," he said enthusiastically. "I'll give you a ring about the children when we plan to go out. Thanks again." He held out his hand a second time.

Landis shook it. "Think nothing of it. But please don't mention this conversation to Blair! Okay?"

"I won't."

"Good luck," she added. And made a hasty escape.

EIGHTEEN

The rest of the week of October 28 was filled with business activity for Landis, Blair, and Lauren. Two tragedies and their occupation with Blair's little fling had taken a tremendous toll on sales as well as on the procurement of listings. For Washburn the week was mainly devoted to helping schedule meetings between witnesses and the commonwealth attorney, who needed to interview them for his preliminary hearing preparation: meetings that included Nelson and Albemarle County deputies who had been involved in the investigations, the hunter Bob "Big Buck" Herman, the coroner, and lab techs, among others. He also met with other Albemarle deputies and Charlottesville police who were concluding their investigation of the time-line on Netherdon's activities in the Charlottesville area on October 9. They promised that a list of names and addresses for subpoena purposes would be faxed to Washburn by Friday.

Bob Herman called Blair Thursday to tell her he had been served a subpoena to testify at the preliminary hearing.

"Reckon I'll be as nervous on the stand as a toad in a nest of snakes," he professed.

"Ow-oh, Bob, what a terrible analogy! You know how I hate snakes. But that aside, you'll do fine," Blair assured him. She didn't dare add that he would no doubt entertain the whole courtroom with his colorful colloquialisms. His tendency to show off didn't need any encouragement.

"Yeh, yeh . . . so you say," Herman scoffed. He fell silent for a few beats, then spoke in a downshifted tone. "Blair, there's something funny about Netherdon's behavior—odd—but I haven't put my finger on it yet. And it bothers me."

"Why?"

"'Cause I think we're missing something in our case."

Wow! *Our* case now?

"Like what, Bob? I don't follow."

"His secretiveness. Well, he's had that all along, but now, in addition, he's acting so abrupt—so angry."

"Don't you think that could be attributed to the church's rejection of him?" Blair asked to nudge the conversation along. Her curiosity was suddenly aroused. Maybe she could learn something to pass on to Landis. Poor Landis . . . she wanted so desperately to get into the investigation, Blair knew.

"Somewhat, maybe. But I feel like it's something besides that. I think he's hiding something."

"Good heavens, Bob, if he *is* the one who killed Bert and stuck Lauren in that shack to die, I guess he's trying to hide his *guilt*!"

"Yes, Blair, granted. But if you could have *seen* him, *heard* him, you'd know what I'm trying to say."

"Okay, Bob, for the sake of discussion, let's agree that there is something else. Something he's hiding. What are some possibilities we can list?"

"Bert might have known or had something she could threaten him with, threaten a future pastorship for him maybe."

"Okay, that would go to motive, too, in addition to revenge for being rejected. Bob, what if someone *else* is involved in the murder with him?"

"Now, *that's* the kind of thing I was wondering about! Or maybe that he's *covering* for someone else," Bob suggested excitedly.

"An interesting possibility. But who?"

"No idea. He's such a close-mouthed, arrogant little—"

"Careful, Bob. Your wife doesn't want you cussing, remember. By the way, how do you know Netherdon so well? You couldn't have heard him preach more than once or twice."

"He's in my Moose Lodge—rather, *was* my lodge. I dropped out because of him and another as . . . . , I mean 'ashcan' just like him!" he finished, having awkwardly substituted *ashcan* for what he really wanted to call the man.

"Well, that certainly answers my question! So, do you know of any close friends he has?"

"Hell no. Hasn't got any. Men don't like him."

"What about women?"

"Oh, yeah, he's had women, all right! Some probably even cared about him. Don't know how close he felt to any of them, though. I'm not sure the bas . . . . uh, the jerk has ever really cared about anybody but himself."

"What women are you talking about?"

"The guys at the lodge said they were what the politically correct now call 'escorts'. Mostly in Charlottesville. And we know he was seeing a widow in Scottsville while his wife was ill, long before she died."

"Damn. The sick hypocrite! I'm now prouder than ever of Bert and our other church board members for rejecting him!"

"You bet! He would have ruined the church. I mean, people would have stopped attending."

A question hit Blair's mind. "Bob, did you tell this stuff to Ned Washburn?"

"I sure did."

"Good," she acknowledged half-heartedly.

Blair bit off saying "great", out of disappointment. For a moment she thought she'd found an area for Landis to pursue. She could just picture Landis dressing up as a pros . . . an "escort"—and setting out to interview Charlottesville's "trade"!

"Bob, I've got to run, get ready to go out. Richard is taking me to dinner and a play in Lynchburg this evening. If you think of anything else, though, give me a buzz, hear. Meanwhile, don't worry about testifying. You'll do great."

"Thanks."

Blair was still a little in shock, although it had been nearly twenty-four hours since Richard had rushed excitedly into her home office and boyishly extended his "invitation" for dinner at The Depot and a performance at Renaissance Theatre. More surprising, he had arranged for Landis to babysit the children! She couldn't help being touched and excited. It had been a very long time since she and Richard had been out on an official date.

On Tuesday he had taken all of them at the office—her, Landis, Lauren, and a temp—to lunch at Travelers Restaurant in Amherst. And in the afternoon he had shopped for nifty new clothes!

Wednesday morning, after the children left for school, he had brought a cup of heavily creamed coffee to her in the bedroom, just as she was walking out of the bathroom wearing a shorty belted robe and carrying a king-size towel. She had propped herself on the bed against a stack of pillows and patted the side of the bed for him to sit beside her. Immediately he had tickled the bottom of her foot nearest him, causing her to spill coffee on the front of her robe. Amid her squeals, he had yanked off her robe, thrown the towel over her, and begun tossing her about as he patted her front to soak up the hot liquid, inadvertently continuing to tickle her. They had both broken into playful laughter at that point. Then he had lifted the towel away and looked at her naked body. Desire had flared in his eyes, abruptly killing his laughter. Slowly, sensually, he had sipped remaining droplets of creamy coffee off her stomach and breasts, trailing his tongue upward to her lips. She had responded, kissing his mouth . . . his face . . . his neck . . . then caressing his nipples. When he threw off his bathrobe and entered her, she had literally hollered her delight. For the first time in six months, they had made love passionately, with abandonment—like they had done in the early years. Just before his strokes lost momentum, she had rolled him over, and, astride, reached orgasm with him. They had lain spent, sated—until desire flared again and they repeated their performance.

Blair felt hot now recalling it.

Thursday morning, today, he had washed breakfast dishes and taken out trash as he left for work. And now, this evening, a dinner and theatre date coming up! What in the world could have prompted such a change in lackadaisical Richard, she wondered.

"Oh no!" she exclaimed abruptly. "Could he have heard something? Figured it out himself?" Her heart pounded a minute before she could breathe regularly, could rationalize. "Ah no . . . no . . . no way. He wouldn't be acting like *this*! He would be hurt . . . be brooding," she continued talking aloud, convincing herself. "Besides, I haven't *actually* cheated," she congratulated herself.

Washburn was disturbed by the reports faxed from Charlottesville and Albemarle investigators Friday. The timeline of the minister's activities was now narrowed more than earlier evidenced, meaning that Netherdon would have had less time to get back to Nelson County to commit a murder and a kidnapping.

Did Netherdon indeed not have enough time? If not, then who? What other someone who could have used the Durango—or conspired with Netherdon to do the deeds? Perplexing. And worrisome—for getting an indictment against Netherdon the following week.

Once again he opened the case file and, starting from the beginning, reviewed all the reports: on interviews, on forensics, on the coroner's exam, on photos. Everything from scratch. The prelim would start Tuesday, whether he was ready or not.

After studying the file, Washburn slumped in his desk chair, scratched his head, and then rested his chin on laced fingers. For the next half hour he pondered the hefty load on his plate for the immediate future: conclusion of the Dumond-Michaels investigation and prelim testimony, development of the relationship with Blair, and career planning.

NINETEEN

Blair arrived first at their designated meeting place in Lynchburg Saturday: O'Charley's Restaurant on Wards Road. She parked and waited in her car until she saw Washburn drive into the lot, then got out and walked toward his car. He was startled by her tapping on his window.

"Hey, where'd you come from?" he asked when his window was still powering down. "I didn't see your car."

"Over there," she replied, pointing to the front parking area.

"I'll move it to the back lot so it won't be conspicuously abandoned," he proposed, opening his door and reaching for her keys.

"Ned, can we go inside for coffee?"

"Sure thing."

Blair asked the hostess for the smoking area. When they were seated in a booth, she immediately lighted a cigarette.

Washburn studied her face. "Something's wrong, isn't it," he stated rather than asked. In the parking lot he had been too excited seeing her to notice that she was nervous. Her asking to get coffee rather than moving her car and going on to Roanoke in his car was certainly a clue he should have detected. But now her smoking in his presence for the very first time was a clue that smacked him in the face.

Blair waited for the waiter to serve their coffees before she spoke. "I can't go," she said simply, her voice flat. "I'm sorry."

"You mean something's come up—" he began.

"No, Ned," she said, stopping what else he might have said in protest. She covered his hand with hers and for the first time raised her eyes to look at him directly. "I mean I can't go to Roanoke with you because I can't continue going out with you. At all."

"Blair! Why?"

"I felt that you would press me to go to a motel, maybe stay the night with you in Roanoke."

"But if I didn't?"

"I'm sorry, Ned. I don't want to hurt you. As I told you last Saturday, I like you. Very much. And I admit I've been very attracted to you—enough to let myself go too far with this as it is. But I can't go further. I don't want an affair, don't want to leave my husband and family. So I must stop seeing you—other than for casual or business reasons. Please say you understand. This isn't easy for me, Ned . . . isn't going to be easy for a long while either."

Ned Washburn swallowed, then cleared his throat. For a long moment he just studied her face. As if preoccupied in thought, he picked up her hand, held it between both of his, gently stroking the wrist.

"Blair, I do understand," he began softly, "and I'm sorry, too. Another time, another place . . . maybe—"

"Yes . . . maybe," she echoed in a near-whisper.

"Sorry, too, if I pushed you—"

"No, no, you didn't! It was . . . chemistry. For us both."

"I hope things will be okay for you—at home and all."

"Better than okay, Ned. This . . . with you . . . has caused . . . will cause a renewal—"

"Then great! Sounds like I've done you some good after all," he said, letting her hand go and trying to chuckle. "Waiter. Over here," he called suddenly to the young man who had brought them coffee.

"Yes, sir?"

"Got a wife or girlfriend?"

"Wife. Been married three weeks."

"Working tonight?"

"No sir. Why?" The waiter was becoming a little uncomfortable, not following this customer's line of questioning.

"Here. Take these tickets. Surprise your new wife this evening," he said, handing over the two concert tickets he had pulled from his inside jacket pocket.

The waiter took them hesitantly, a look of incredulity on his face that quickly transformed into gleeful enthusiasm when he saw what they were.

"Wow! Neat!" he exclaimed. "You sure you want to give them away? It's not some kind of joke?"

"No, son, it's not a joke," Washburn said, a note of resignation in his voice. "We've just learned we can't go. Have fun."

Thanking him effusively, the waiter departed to spread the news among his co-workers.

"Ned, let me pay for the tickets, please. It's the very least I can do for ruining—"

"Absolutely not," he interrupted. "But thanks for offering. Now let's get out of here."

Washburn walked Blair to her car, opened the door, and motioned her to slip behind the wheel. When she was seated and buckled up, he reached for her left hand and kissed its back. Still holding her hand, he said, "Be happy, Blair. See you." He dropped her hand, shut the door firmly, and walked away toward his car without looking back.

Blair drove quickly to the far side of the next-door business to be out of Washburn's sight and parked long enough to tissue away her tears. Then she turned into the heavy traffic of Wards Road and headed home.

"Well, at least you made it back!" Lauren greeted Blair as she walked into the office kitchen Monday morning. "How *was* the hot date?"

"I didn't go."

"Didn't go where?" Landis asked, walking in as Blair spoke.

"To Roanoke. With Ned."

"Well, hells bells! Why not? What happened?" Landis asked in surprise.

"I met him in Lynchburg as planned. And told him I couldn't go."

"Yah . . . I got that part! Question was, why?" Landis taunted.

"Because I didn't want to! Okay?" Blair flared back, near tears.

"Hey, hey," Lauren cooed to Blair. "It's okay. Landis didn't mean anything. We're just curious, is all."

"Get me a coffee, and I'll try to tell ya'll," Blair bargained, and proceeded to sit down at the kitchen table.

For the next fifteen minutes they sat at the table and let Blair talk without interrupting her. When it appeared she had finished, both Lauren and Landis moved to hug her tightly. Seated again, Lauren was the first to respond to Blair's confession.

"I think you made a wise decision, Blair, though I'm sure it was difficult, to say the least. And we're proud of you. Can you share what decided you to break it off now?"

Blair looked at her two friends for long moments before deciding to answer.

Finally, she began tentatively. "Well, last week Richard made . . . I mean, he did so many sweet things just for me . . . like right out of the blue . . . and took me on a date . . . and, well, was suddenly just so tender and loving that our relationship was renewed. Back like it used to be. Better, actually." She stopped talking and stared across the room, dreamy-eyed.

Lauren looked at Landis questioningly. Landis returned her a very exaggerated wink.

"It hurts, though," Blair resumed. "Because I care about Ned a lot. Love for my family is stronger, so I had to end seeing him. The stress, and the risks, are just too great. The past month has been an emotional roller coaster. Of ecstasy and misery. But, although I had been tempted before last week, I probably always knew that when decision-time arrived I just wouldn't be able to handle an affair."

Neither Lauren nor Landis said a word, just smiled. Blair whirled on Landis.

"You're wanting to say 'I told you so', aren't you?"

"I'm not saying anything."

"But you're dying to! So go ahead. SAY IT!"

TWENTY

The preliminary hearing opened in General District Court Tuesday morning at 9:30, with Judge Rowland Garnett presiding.

Della Dumond Shales was called to the stand as the first witness. Commonwealth Attorney Paul Parker's questions walked her through a description and timeline of her mother's activities on October 9, ending with an account of Della's unanswered calls to her mother and later discovery of her mother's disappearance from her home.

Next C.A. Parker called Toni Mathieson, a member of the board of trustees at Roberta Dumond's church, to establish that the board had rejected Netherdon's application under the direct guidance of Chairperson Dumond. Thus motive was introduced.

The coroner testified regarding cause and time of Mrs. Dumond's death and location of her body discovery.

The defense attorney elected not to cross-examine the first three witnesses.

Ned Washburn was the fourth witness sworn in. "Good morning, officer. Please state your name and position." When Washburn had done so, the C.A. continued. "How did your investigation initially connect Clovis Netherdon to Mrs. Dumond's death?" he asked.

"Tire treads. Prints photographed and molded at Mrs. Dumond's home and at the body site matched the treads on Mr. Netherdon's Dodge Durango."

"What connected him to the kidnapping of Lauren Michaels?"

"Same thing. Photos and molds of tire prints at the property from which Ms. Michaels was kidnapped, as well as molds and photos of prints found at the shack where she was imprisoned, matched the Durango tire treads. And a broken light lens—"

"And what subsequent evidence, if any, connects Mr. Netherdon to the crimes?" the C.A. continued, ignoring reference to the lens they had not corroborated.

"Hair found in the Durango was Mrs. Dumond's, and blood found in it was from Ms. Michaels. Tissue and blood found on the discarded tire iron are a mixture from the two women."

"Discarded tire iron?"

"Yes. It was found by hunters, near the shack where Lauren Michaels was imprisoned."

"Thank you, Mr. Washburn. Judge, I submit photos of the tire marks and mold casts labeled by location of discovery, photos of tires on Mr. Netherdon's Durango, and lab reports on them as well as on the forensic evidence referenced by Officer Washburn. Your witness, counselor," the C.A. said to defense attorney Terry Bagley from Charlottesville, then returned to the prosecutor's table.

"Officer Washburn, how many vehicles in Nelson County have tires with the same tread design as Mr. Netherdon's?" Bagley challenged right off.

"I don't know."

"How many vehicles were examined during the investigation?"

"One hundred, forty-three."

"How many had the same tread design as Mr. Netherdon's Durango?"

"Ten."

"Oh! Ten, huh? On what basis did you rule out the other nine?"

"Only the tires on the Durango had the exact depth of tread as the photographed and molded prints."

"And you determined that with your naked eye?"

"No. Lab tests did. Reports were just submitted to the court."

"All right, Officer Washburn, to another matter. You said 'found in the Durango' in reference to hair and blood. Who found these things?"

"Deputy Joe Brown, Deputy Orieman Taskell, and I saw the hair and stains in the Durango and discovered the tire iron missing when we searched it Monday, October 14, after obtaining a warrant. I impounded the vehicle. A forensics team collected samples."

"Did you touch the evidence?"

"No."

"Did the two deputies touch it?"

"No."

"How did the vehicle get from Mr. Netherdon's residence to the forensics team?"

"Rollback wrecker."

"Did you accompany it?"

"No."

"Well, Officer Washburn, the chain of custody of that evidence was compromised—the evidence contaminated. Right?"

"I don't think so."

"But you don't know for sure, do you?"

"No."

"Thank you! As to the tire iron 'found' by hunters, did they touch it?"

"They said they didn't. It was in a plastic grocery bag."

"Found indoors?"

"No. Outside, in tangled vines."

"So! Exposed to the elements, handled by hunters. It, too, could have been contaminated, right?"

"Yes, but—"

"Thank you, officer. No further questions."

Lauren was called to the stand and asked by the commonwealth attorney to describe the time, location, and details of her abduction. "Your witness, counselor," C.A. Parker concluded, turning her over to the defense.

"Did you *see* your abductor, Ms. Michaels?" defense attorney Bagley asked in cross-examination.

"No."

"Did you *hear* your abductor say anything?"

"No."

"Then you can't say that it *was* Mr. Netherdon, can you?"

"No," Lauren acknowledged.

"Thank you, Ms. Michaels," Bagley smirked.

"Can't say it *wasn't* either," Lauren added saucily, just as the attorney turned away dismissively.

A one-note chuckle ran through the courtroom spectators. The C.A.'s dimples deepened and a twinkle shone in the judge's eyes momentarily.

"You may step down, Ms. Michaels," Judge Garnett instructed. Landis and Blair high-fived Lauren as she stepped down from the witness stand.

Called as the next witness, Bob Herman, the "big buck" hunter, further entertained the gallery. "Howdy, judge," he greeted as he approached the witness chair. The judge nodded, almost imperceptively, but said nothing.

Capturing Herman's attention quickly, C.A. Parker asked him to identify himself first and then describe details of his role in the search for Lauren and his role in her recovery.

"How was her imprisonment in the shack secured?" Parker asked in conclusion of his questioning.

"A four-foot-long board, two by six inches in size and mounted on steel brackets, was across the only door. No windows in the place."

"Any way she could have escaped?"

"Absolutely not. She would have died there."

"Thank you, Mr. Herman. Mr. Bagley may have questions for you."

"Good morning, sir," Bagley greeted as he approached the witness.

"Believe it's afternoon now. Leastways, my stomach says it is," Herman retorted, a bemused expression on his face.

The spectators twittered. Those who knew Herman were concerned that such a reception might encourage him to ham it up too much.

"Well, so it is," the defense attorney conceded sarcastically. Composing himself with effort, Bagley continued. "Mr. Herman, you found the tire mark or marks at the shack where you found Ms. Michaels, correct?"

"No, I didn't."

"Then who?"

"Another hunter. Ross Peters."

"Did either of you disturb the marks before officers arrived?"

"No, sir!"

"When did you find the tire iron?"

"I didn't. Two of my hunt club friends found it a week later."

"Ah ha! No one saw it the week before?"

"No."

"Then it could have been planted there later, correct?"

"Not hardly."

"But you don't know for sure, do you?"

"No. But neither do you!"

"Just answer the questions you're asked, Mr. Herman," the judge instructed.

"Mr. Herman, when you arrived at the shack October 13 was the board on the outside of the door?" Bagley demanded, unfortunately speaking before recovering from his annoyance with the witness.

Herman huffed a breath of air audibly, staring blankly ahead for a second before turning an incredulous expression to the judge.

"Judge, what kind of a stupid ques—"

"Answer the question, Mr. Herman. If you can," the judge interposed.

"You bet I can, Judge," Herman granted emphatically. Turning back to face the artless defense attorney, he spoke as if explaining to a child. "You see, Mr. Bagley, when you're outside your house you couldn't turn the dead-bolt lock that's inside. Right? You would—"

"Your Honor?" Attorney Bagley pleaded.

"That's enough, Mr. Herman."

"Yes, Your Honor," Bob Herman said soberly. "The board was on the outside of the door, Mr. Bagley. Ms. Michaels was inside the building."

"Thank you for that!" Bagley snipped. "Now, you see Clovis Netherdon sitting over there. He's not a young man nor a big man. Do you think he's strong enough to render an adult woman unconscious, load and unload her from a huge vehicle, transport her into that building you've described, and then lift such a board to lock her in?"

"I haven't the faintest idea."

"No further questions for this witness," Bagley scoffed.

"You may step down, Mr. Herman," the judge directed.

"With pleasure!" Herman said exasperatedly.

Last on the witness stand for the commonwealth attorney were two lab technicians. In response to the C.A.'s questions, one of them utilized a projection screen to show the photos as he described the techniques for determining the depth of tread on a real tire and in a mold cast of a soil imprint. The second technician explained the analysis of hair, blood, and tissue.

Defense attorney Bagley posed only one question. "Could you determine if any of the evidence you handled had been contaminated or not in its collection or transport?" he asked the tech who had presented the analysis of hair, blood, and tissue.

"No," the tech conceded.

"No further questions, Your Honor."

"Do you have other witnesses? Anything else?" Judge Garnett asked the commonwealth attorney.

"No, Your Honor."

Judge Garnett looked at his watch. "I have commitments for the rest of the afternoon, so court is recessed until tomorrow morning at 9:30," he announced and gavelled the session to a close.

Lauren, Landis, and Blair had sat in the next-to-last row on the right side of the courtroom, Lauren sitting next to the aisle. Washburn sat in the aisle seat behind her. They all remained seated while the courtroom emptied, curious to observe the variety of people attending.

"What's wrong, Lauren?" Landis asked, rising from her seat and noticing that Lauren was still sitting, elbow on her knee and chin resting on a fist.

"Oh, nothing's wrong," Lauren responded quickly, losing her frown of concentration. "I just smelled something."

"You mean somebody far—"

"Heavens no, Landis! No, this was a scent that stirred a memory . . . an association of some kind . . . something that bothers me. I just can't place what it is."

"Hey, Washburn, wait up!" Landis shouted. Washburn was walking to the well of the courtroom, where two deputies stood talking. Landis's shout stopped him in mid-stride. He turned and walked back.

"What in the world, woman?" he chastised her.

"Something you ought'ta hear. Lauren, tell him what you just said."

Lauren repeated her experience.

"What kind of smell?" Washburn asked.

"I don't know. It was a fleeting sensation that hit me after the crowd moved past."

"But you think it's significant in some way?"

"Definitely."

"Well, tell you what. Come back tomorrow morning, move about the courtroom as much as you can, see if you can detect it specifically. Okay?"

"Sure." It was easy to be agreeable; Lauren was planning to return the next day anyway. So were Landis and Blair.

"See ya'll tomorrow then," Washburn said and walked away.

"Suppose he's angry with you, Blair?" Lauren asked. "He seemed kinda cool and distant."

"Not angry. Not exactly distant either. He's putting on a formal front . . . being business-like. Trying to make things easier for both of us, I think," Blair equivocated.

"Whatever, you have to give it to him. He's a gentleman!" Lauren praised assertively.

"Lauren," Landis commanded, bringing their attention back to 'sleuthing' business. "The odor you smelled . . . could it have been shaving lotion? I smelled that when Bob Herman and another man walked past us."

"I don't think so. But if it was shaving lotion, the point is that there's a *particular association* with the odor . . . the scent! It niggled at my mind for a split second, but so far I haven't pinpointed it."

"You said he was the first person you saw—smelled—when he opened that stinky shack," Landis offered, "so I just thought maybe—"

"And good thinking, too," Blair chimed in. "I doubt Bob is coming back tomorrow, though. Probably got a bellyful today. But I'll ask him for a dab of his brand and bring it back with me so you can whiff it up close."

"Okay, pals, that's all we can do today. SO . . . let's hit Vito's for a *rather* late lunch," Landis proposed.

TWENTY-ONE

The next morning Lauren did her "sniff test" as unobtrusively as she could. She arrived at the courthouse early, deposited her purse and jacket on a seat in mid-room, then returned to the hallway to stand at the top of the stairs and pretend to be waiting for someone. From that vantage point she nonchalantly observed people arriving, her flared nostrils poised for activity. At 9:25, with ninety-five percent of the courtroom filled, Lauren abandoned her post. Sniffing out a solitary late arrival would be entirely too obvious. Landis and Blair were in seats beside her reserved one, and she joined them a minute before the court session was called to order.

"Did you smell the scent?" Blair asked.

"Nope."

"Here, take a whiff of this," Blair directed, uncapping and holding a small bottle to Lauren's nose. It contained a sample of Bob Herman's shaving lotion.

Lauren inhaled deeply. "Is that it?" Landis whispered.

"No."

"Are you sure?" Blair insisted.

"Positive!" Lauren asserted.

"Interesting," Landis mused, her mental wheels turning again, trying to birth some other sleuthing activity.

Judge Garnett had perused the photos and lab reports and listened carefully to the commonwealth attorney's examination and the defense attorney's cross-examination of witnesses on Tuesday. Afterward he had noted that the defense had so far produced nothing to raise reasonable doubt. Indeed, the commonwealth's case appeared to be strong enough to be sent on to circuit court for trial. However, the defense had witnesses to call, so he maintained an open mind as court reconvened Wednesday.

The first witness called by defense attorney Terry Bagley was the church superintendent, Atwood Bland.

Washburn turned around in his seat two rows in front of Blair, Landis, and Lauren and winked at them. They nodded their understanding that the defense intended to lay out a timeline to alibi Netherdon for the day of the crimes. But, based on the information Washburn had gathered, they thought it couldn't be done. Although Washburn had shared his concern about the Albemarle investigators' report, the women still believed Netherdon had had enough time to return from Charlottesville, abduct Roberta Dumond to kill later, and to be hiding at the Bannister property at 3:00. The Albemarle report had Netherdon still in Charlottesville at 1:30, making the timeline tight but certainly possible.

Superintendent Bland testified to exactly what he had told Washburn. Netherdon had been in his office on October 9 from 10:00 to 11:10 a.m. Commonwealth Attorney Parker elected not to cross-examine.

Next, Netherdon's attorney called a woman to the stand. She was forty-five to fifty, slightly plump, dressed in a navy blue business suit.

"State your name, occupation, and address for the court," Attorney Bagley directed her.

"Frances Newell, proprietor of Fran's Massage Salon, Charlottesville," she replied in a throaty, sensual voice.

There were several audible "ah's" scattered throughout the courtroom.

"Is an escort service a part of your business, too?" Bagley asked.

"On occasion."

"Such as?"

"Conventions, professional dinners."

"Do you ever provide escorts to individuals for private affairs?"

"Depends," she drawled.

Bagley declined to pursue her answer, already regretting wading in too deep. "Do you know my client, Clovis Netherdon?" he asked instead, to move on to the purpose for calling her.

"Yes, of course."

"In what capacity?"

"He's my client, too," she returned, with tongue-in-cheek mischievousness.

"Please explain," Bagley pursued, clearing his throat, fearing he was stepping deeper into dung.

"He comes to my establishment once a week. For a massage, of course."

"Of course! Was he there on October 9, and, if so, at what time?"

"Yes. He arrived at 11:30."

"And left at what time?"

"At 1:30."

"Thank you. No more questions. Your witness, counselor," Bagley said to C.A. Parker.

"Ms. Newell, how long has Mr. Netherdon been a *client*?" the C.A. opened his questioning.

"Two years."

"When he left your place of business on October 9, did he say he was going directly home to Nelson County?"

"No."

"On other visits, did he usually indicate that he was going straight home?"

"Yes, usually."

"Thank you, madam. No further questions."

Slight sounds from the spectators suggested that they had not missed the "madam" pun.

Washburn sighed relief. The 1:30 departure from Ms. Newell's business tallied with the report faxed to him. And he thought the "usually straight home" reference would cement his and the C.A.'s contention that Netherdon had had just enough time to get home and do what he was charged with.

"Next, I call Billy Pitts," Attorney Bagley announced loudly. A lean young man in jeans and a blue shirt was escorted into the courtroom by a deputy and sworn in.

The C.A. glanced quizzically toward Washburn. Washburn shrugged, denoting ignorance of the witness. Landis, Blair, and Lauren looked at each other, concern showing in their eyes. None of them had heard of Pitts as a potential witness either.

"State your name, occupation, and address for the court," Bagley directed.

"Billy Pitts, attendant at Peak's Gas Station, Charlottesville."

"Do you know Clovis Netherdon, Mr. Pitts?"

"Yes, sir."

"Do you see him in the courtroom today?"

"Yes, sir."

"Please point him out."

Billy Pitts identified Netherdon sitting at the defense table, wearing a dark suit and blue shirt.

"In what capacity do you know Mr. Netherdon?"

"He's a regular customer at the gas station."

"By regular, what do you mean? How often does he stop there?"

"Once every week. Occasionally, an extra time."

"The once-a-week visit, is it always the same day of the week?"

"Yes, sir. Wednesday."

"How long has he been a regular customer at your station?"

"I don't remember exactly. Several years, though."

"And you've been employed there all that time?"

"Yes, sir. Been at the station six years."

"Mr. Pitts, was Mr. Netherdon at your gas station Wednesday, October 9?"

"Yes, sir."

"At what time?"

"At 2:15."

A gasp escaped Landis, Blair, and Lauren. Washburn's shoulders slumped. If this testimony was true, their theory was totally shot down. No way could the man have driven to Roberta Dumond's home and then backtracked fifteen miles to the Bannister property in forty-five minutes!

"How can you be sure of the time, Mr. Pitts?"

Washburn's interest was piqued. Maybe there *was* hope.

"Credit card record. Mr. Netherdon always leaves his receipts on the counter, but I pick them up and hold them for thirty days—in case he should question charges when he gets his monthly statement in the mail."

"And is *this* the receipt for October 9?" Bagley held a gas credit card receipt in front of the witness. "Showing the date and exact time of purchase?"

"Yes, sir, it is," Pitts acknowledged.

Bagley handed the receipt to the judge and a copy of it to the commonwealth attorney. Hope vanquished, Washburn bowed his head.

"Thank you, Mr. Pitts. Oh, by the way, what vehicle was Mr. Netherdon driving on October 9?" Bagley asked, displaying a snide smile.

"A Ford Escort."

It was plain to see that Terry Bagley had enjoyed delivering the last thrust to the Nelson County prosecution.

"Thank you, Mr. Pitts. No further questions from me," Bagley asserted, again grinning his triumph.

When the C.A. remained sitting, the judge addressed him. "Counselor, do you wish to cross?"

"Uh . . . Your Honor, may be have a recess at this juncture?" C.A. Parker asked, clearly needing to buy time for re-grouping.

Judge Garnett frowned, but checked his watch. "Well, all right. Let's take fifteen minutes."

The judge was barely off the bench when the commonwealth attorney huddled with Washburn. Landis, Blair, and Lauren made a dash for the corridor, thinking Washburn was following. They knew the case was in a pickle, very likely going to be thrown out. Maybe somehow they and Washburn could come up with a strategy to stall the hearing until they could investigate further.

The three women stood in the corridor just outside the rear side door to the courtroom, talking in low tones among themselves. A number of people walked past them to the end of the corridor to get a drink of water or to use the restrooms or to just chat. Several walked past with a cigarette and lighter in hand, preparing to go outside for a quick smoke. Suddenly a woman wearing a scarf tied over her head rushed from the courtroom's front side door and stalked past them, bumping Lauren's elbow in the process.

"THAT'S IT! PERFUME!" Lauren shouted, pointing to the woman's retreating back. Landis and Blair turned just in time to catch a glimpse of the woman's backside as she turned the corner leading to the stairway.

"What do you mean, Lauren?" Landis demanded. Five people who had been standing nearby approached them, alerted by Lauren's shout.

"I know now . . . the scent I was trying to remember . . . it was perfume like that woman is wearing. I smelled it the second before I was hit at the Bannister property!"

"Oh, my God, you think—" Blair began.

"Stay with her, Blair!" Landis commanded, already running toward the courtroom door. "I'll get Washburn," she called over her shoulder. That was her second instinct. Her first had been to chase after the perfumed woman.

Washburn, who was still talking with the commonwealth attorney, saw Landis hustling down the aisle toward him and rose from his chair to intercept her. Her manner spelled urgency. He knew her well enough to know something serious was behind it.

The commonwealth attorney sensed it, too, and, thinking it could be something personal, rose to move away from the table.

"No, stay!" Landis pleaded. "You need to hear this, too, and there's little time to consider it."

Washburn pulled a chair back from the table for her. "Lauren Michaels just identified the scent she detected here yesterday. It's a perfume worn by a woman who just stalked out past us. Lauren says she remembers smelling it at the Bannister property a split second before she was knocked unconscious!" Landis gushed, before having to stop to catch her breath.

"Landis! What did she look like?" Washburn beseeched.

"Didn't see her face. But she was wearing a tweed coat and a scarf-like thing wound around her head."

"A turban! I saw her, too. And I know who she is!" Washburn exploded. A scenario suddenly burned in his head. "Paul, you've got to ask Judge Garnett for a continuance," he pressed, anxiety and excitement firing him to jump up and prepare to leave.

"Hell, man, I want to ask—*need* to ask for a continuance! But you gotta give me something to support the request," C.A. Parker implored.

"Tell him that investigators," Washburn paused to wink at Landis, "have uncovered additional evidence very relevant to the case and that you need at least another day to prepare for rebuttal. Will that work?" Washburn summarized.

"You bet! I'll ask for continuance until Friday. And I'll decline a cross of the Pitts fella. Get back to me just as soon as you can, you hear!"

"I promise. Now I gotta go!" Washburn said, flashing a radiant smile as he picked up his file folder and strode a few yards to the door.

"Whoa, Ned! Hold it a sec!" Landis barked from the courtroom well. He stopped and waited just outside the door for her to catch up to him. "I got something else . . . thought it best not to give it to you in front of Paul Parker."

"What, for heavens' sake?" he asked impatiently.

"Here," Landis said, as she tore a page from a small memo book and handed it to him. He looked at it, then back to Landis.

"Invoice number 0402196. And a phone number. What's your point?"

"Call West End Dodge in Richmond, at that number. Ask the body shop service manager to pull up that invoice and tell you if there's a license tag number or vehicle identification number on it. When he told me they had replaced a lens on a three-year-old Dodge Durango on October 10th, I asked only if there was a name. There wasn't. The invoice was just labeled cash. So I didn't pursue it, dammit! But maybe that woman—"

"Gal, if this pans out, you definitely get the award for 'Outstanding Sleuth of the Year'!" Washburn gushed, as he hugged her tightly. "And I might just forego bawling you out for sneaking into the investigation against my instructions," he added teasingly. "At least you brought this to me rather than giving chase yourself!"

"Don't think I didn't fight the temptation!"

"Seriously, Landis, thanks once again for rescuing me. I'll be in touch soon," he concluded soberly, patted her on the back, and took off running.

TWENTY-TWO

Washburn called West End Dodge, then sought a subpoena for the body shop manager's appearance in court Friday. That having been quickly arranged, he headed off to the Howardsville area of Nelson County.

Driving faster than he should on winding Route 56 East, Washburn still managed to focus on the case. A memory from the first days of the investigation had returned with a jolt: his visit to the Millard home and Shirley Millard's attitude. She had been sullen, uncooperative. At the time he had wondered if she was retarded, bi-polar, or just plain mean. He had had no reason to think she was hiding something, might indeed be involved in the crimes. Particularly considering how open and friendly her husband Randy had been.

Now a scenario was playing in his mind: Shirley Millard was in a relationship with Netherdon, no doubt fancying herself in love with him. On his behalf, probably to revenge his rejection by the church, and, with or without his knowledge or help, she had killed Roberta

Dumond. Somehow Lauren had been an accidental connection. Washburn puzzled over that once again.

The Millards' home was a half-dozen miles or more west of the Bannister property where Lauren had been abducted, and Mrs. Dumond's home was more than a half dozen miles beyond the Millards. The Bannister house was vacant, had only a few pieces of furniture on the second floor.

"Ah ha!" Washburn said aloud. "A bed! I bet Millard and Netherdon were using that place as their rendezvous for sex!"

"Why would she have been there that Wednesday, though, and needing to hide?" his self-questioning continued. "Planning to dispose of Mrs. Dumond's body there perhaps? She *was* familiar with the property—might have figured it to be a safe place to stash a body or more probably to bury it."

As he neared the spot where Mrs. Dumond's body had been found, the puzzle solidified in his mind.

"That's it! If she had *planned* to dump the body beside the creek, she wouldn't have needed to go on to the Bannister property. She dumped it later—after Lauren walked in on her and necessitated a change in plans."

The whole murder-kidnapping scenario was certainly convoluted, Washburn acknowledged. There could be only one explanation for such a scattered, nonsensical crime scene. And it wasn't panic, he calculated, but very simply the work of mental instability. Maybe even insanity. Hearing testimony in court that the man for whom she had killed had been unfaithful to her all along must have provoked the jealous fury in Shirley Millard that sent her stomping angrily from the courtroom, leaving behind the scent of suspicion that would nail her.

With that impression clearly stamped in his mind, Washburn drove into the Millards' yard. Randy was loading firewood on his pick-up truck.

"Hey, Mr. Washburn," he called out, and walked briskly forward to intercept the officer.

They exchanged pleasantries and small talk, a regular rural custom, for several minutes before Washburn got down to business.

"Is Mrs. Millard home?"

"Sure. Want me to call her out?"

"No. Not yet. I want to ask you some questions first."

"All right. Shoot," Randy Millard invited in his usual heartily friendly manner, and rested his hips against a front fender of the cruiser.

"Randy, back on Wednesday, October 9, the day you took a load of logs to North Garden, was Mrs. Millard at home when you returned?"

Millard lifted his cap and scratched his head, studying the ground for a moment. "Naw, she won't. She came home around six-thirty. I remember because she was in a real snit all right. Snapped my head off when I asked what was for supper. Said she didn't feel good and if I wanted supper I could just fix it myself or I could go to Lumpkins Restaurant in Scottsville. Didn't say another word."

"Does she know Clovis Netherdon?"

"Hell, yes! Talks about the sucker all the time. Me, I got no use for him!"

"What does she say about him?"

"That he's so *good* to her, that he *understands* her, that they're *soul mates*," Randy Millard mimicked his wife. "Stuff like that. Me? Huump . . . treats me like I'm the rear end of a horse. Calls me one, too. And she don't say it that nice neither!" he declared.

Washburn believed him. He hadn't forgotten her coldness and belligerence on his first visit to the Millards.

"Has she ever used Netherdon's Durango?"

"Yeah. All the time."

"Do you know if she used it that particular Wednesday?"

"No, I don't."

"What about the day following? Thursday, October 10?"

"Oh, yeah! Gone all day long that day. Said she was running *errands* for Netherdon," Randy jeered.

"Brace yourself, Randy. There's going to be some unpleasant business, I'm afraid. Come on, let's go inside," Washburn coaxed gently, and nudged Randy's arm in a companionable gesture. He felt genuine sorrow for the man.

Washburn walked into the kitchen behind Randy Millard. Shirley was sitting at the table, idly thumbing a deck of cards and sipping coffee from a mug. Washburn saw the scene as a pose, a show of indifference; he had no doubt that she had been aware of his arrival on the property fifteen minutes earlier.

What did surprise him was that she was not wearing the turban. Nor anything on her head. Nearly two inches of gray hair showed above her scalp; beyond that, dull reddish-colored hair hung limply to below her collar.

She looked up as Washburn stepped around Randy. Her gaze was blank, her face expressionless. She said nothing.

Washburn moved quickly to the back of her chair. "Please stand, Mrs. Millard," he commanded.

Zombie-like, she stood. With a flash of metal, Washburn had her cuffed before her husband realized what was happening. "Mrs. Millard, you're under arrest—" he began.

"What's going on here? You think—" Randy blurted, interrupting, then stopped short as the reality began to sink in.

"—for involvement in the murder of Roberta Dumond and the abduction of Lauren Michaels," Washburn resumed, then proceeded to Mirandize her.

"Shirley, why?" Randy entreated.

"Oh, shut your stupid face, Randy!" she spat. "I hate you. I hate *all* you stupid men! You just use women—"

"Mrs. Millard, let's go," Washburn cut in. He caught her elbow and steered her toward the back door.

Randy Millard stood rooted, shoulders slumped, his whole body a statement of dejection.

"You gonna be all right, Millard?" Washburn asked, turning to look at Randy before making an exit.

"Yeah. I'll be along shortly. Need to talk—"

"Fine. I'll be in my office."

TWENTY-THREE

When the preliminary hearing was reconvened Friday morning, the defense called Netherdon to the stand. The move surprised the commonwealth attorney because it hadn't seemed necessary after the man's alibi had been factually corroborated, but the C.A. was delighted. It was a perfect set-up for his grilling Netherdon on cross, thus helping to produce a surprise for the minister and his attorney.

It took the defense less than ten minutes to underscore Netherdon's alibi.

"You were in Charlottesville past 2:15 p.m. on October 9, correct?" Terry Bagley opened his questioning.

"Correct."

"Where did you go when you left Charlottesville?"

"Scottsville."

"For what purpose?"

"To meet with the directors at Thacker Brothers Funeral Home."

"Did you meet with them?"

"No. They were not in. But I signed the register and also left a note for the directors, asking them to call me later in the evening."

"And you returned home at what time?"

"A little after 6:00. I attended to some errands and then stopped at the IGA to do some grocery shopping. You've got the receipt."

Bagley ignored the last statement. "Reverend Netherdon, did you have anything to do with the murder of Roberta Dumond and the kidnapping of Lauren Michaels?" he asked bluntly instead.

"Absolutely not!"

"Thank you. No further questions. Your witness, counselor."

Commonwealth Attorney Paul Parker dived right in. "Mr. Netherdon, you told investigating officers that you didn't drive your Durango at all on Wednesday, October 9. Is that correct?"

"Yes."

"Further, you said that no one else used it on October 9. Is that correct?"

"Yes."

"Mr. Netherdon, do you wish to re-consider your answer?"

"Uh . . . what do you mean?"

"Isn't it true that you sometimes let someone else, maybe even others, use it?"

"Well . . . uh . . . from time to time I lend it to friends."

"Friends? Name them."

"That's my private business. I don't have to answer."

"Your Honor—" C.A. Parker implored.

"Answer the question, Mr. Netherdon," Judge Garnett instructed.

"Last year my nephew from Delaware—"

"THIS year, Mr. Netherdon! Particularly October 9. Who used your Durango that day?"

"I don't know. I don't know if anyone did."

"Oh yes, that's right, you were not home. You were in Charlottesville with your . . . what did we hear? Your masseuse, was it? Frances Newell?"

"Yes. And she's also a friend."

"Actually she's more than that to you, right?"

Defense attorney Bagley objected.

"I'll allow it for now," Judge Garnett said, "but get to your point quickly, counselor. Don't go afield too far. Answer the question, Mr. Netherdon," he directed.

"I don't know what you mean," Netherdon returned defensively.

"Yes, you do. And I remind you that you're under oath. Now, again, do you have a more personal relationship with Ms. Newell? A sexual relationship in fact?"

"Yes," Netherdon answered inaudibly.

"Louder, Mr. Netherdon. Speak louder, please," the judge admonished.

"Yes."

Shirley Millard snorted, unable to contain herself. Sitting on the back row, she had been unnoticed by Netherdon. Her snorting sound drew his attention immediately—and that of everyone in the courtroom. Seeing her, Netherdon blanched white.

C.A. Parker went for the jugular. "Do you know Shirley Millard, Mr. Netherdon?"

"Yes."

"Is she a *friend*, too?"

"Yes."

"An intimate friend?"

"I don't understand."

"Well, I'll re-phrase. Are you and Mrs. Millard lovers?"

Gasps erupted throughout the courtroom.

"Judge . . ." Netherdon begged, red-faced.

"Mr. Parker, I admonished you to not go too far afield. Can you demonstrate the relevance of this line of questioning to the charges?"

"Yes, I can, Your Honor. I'm coming right to it."

C.A. Parker knew he had gotten away with eliciting the information about Netherdon's relationship with Frances Newell. That *was* irrelevant to the charges against Netherdon. His motive for getting it out in court was simply to provoke Shirley Millard into implicating Netherdon, if indeed he was involved in the crimes. It was why he had arranged for her to be brought from jail to the courtroom.

"Proceed then. Answer the question, Mr. Netherdon," Judge Garnett prompted.

"Uh . . . we've had a relationship—"

"An affair, more precisely? Rendezvousing at the Bannister property?"

"Yes."

"And you sometimes lend her the Durango?"

"Yes."

"So, Mr. Netherdon, back to my question about October 9. Did Mrs. Millard use the vehicle that day?"

"As I said, I don't know. I wasn't home," he repeated once again.

"But she *could* have used it?"

"Yes. She has a set of keys."

"And you didn't check to see if it had been used? Its condition?"

"No."

"Did Mrs. Millard drive the Durango Thursday, October 10?"

"Yes."

"Do you know where she drove it?"

"Yes. She said she had business in Richmond and needed to take the Durango."

"No further questions at this time, Your Honor, but I reserve the right to recall Mr. Netherdon."

"Very well. Re-direct, Mr. Bagley?

"No, Your Honor."

"You may step down, Mr. Netherdon," the judge directed. "Anything else, counselors?" he asked.

"Not for me, Your Honor," Terry Bagley answered.

"I have one rebuttal witness, Your Honor," C.A. Parker said.

"Call your witness, then, counselor."

"I call Brad Sorensen," Parker announced, turning to nod to a deputy, the signal to fetch the witness.

A stocky man dressed in dark blue pants and a light blue shirt with a name patch over the breast pocket was sworn in and directed to take the stand.

"State your name, occupation, and address, sir," C.A. Paul Parker began his examination of the witness.

"Bradley Sorensen, body shop manager at West End Dodge in Richmond."

"Mr. Sorensen, are you familiar with this document?" Parker asked, holding a paper in front of the witness.

"Yes, sir."

"Will you describe it for the court, please?"

"It's an original invoice from my place of work, West End Dodge."

"Read the description of the service rendered, please."

"Replacement of a parking light lens on the front right side of a Dodge Durango," Sorensen read.

"Is there a customer name on it?"

"No, sir. Just 'cash' on the customer line."

"Why so?"

"It's typically how we handle invoices for minor service on drop-in's."

"I see. However, you noted some kind of identification on this invoice, did you not?"

"Yes, sir. Three ID's. The VIN number, the tag number, the make and model of vehicle."

"VIN is the abbreviation for vehicle identification number, correct?"

"Yes, sir."

"Read both numbers, please. VIN and tag numbers."

The body shop manager read the numbers aloud.

"Mr. Sorensen, I'm handing you a copy of a Virginia vehicle registration card. Please read the highlighted boxes for the court."

Sorensen read the numbers in the highlighted boxes, which were the VIN and license tag numbers.

"The same numbers as on your invoice. Now, read the name on the registration card, please."

"Clovis R. Netherdon," the man read.

"Your Honor, here are copies of the invoice and registration card," C.A. Parker said as he handed the documentation up to the judge.

"You have copies for the defense, too?" Judge Garnett asked.

"Yes." Parker turned and handed the document copies to Terry Bagley.

"Thank you, Mr. Sorensen. No further questions."

"No cross, Your Honor," Bagley stated.

"Your Honor, may I address the court?" C.A. Parker asked.

Judge Garnett nodded assent.

"Your Honor, witness testimony has verified Mr. Netherdon's alibi for Wednesday, October 9. His own testimony here today identifies Shirley Millard as the person who had possession of the Durango vehicle when the lens was replaced on October 10. Her husband has told Investigator Washburn that she was not home Wednesday afternoon, October 9, and also that she drove the Durango to Richmond October 10. In light of this information, the people wish to drop the charges of murder and kidnapping against Clovis Netherdon."

A loud sigh eminated from Netherdon at the defense table.

"However," Parker continued, "we're charging him and Shirley Millard as co-conspirators for the same two crimes."

"Agreed. Defendants are remanded. This case is dismissed," Judge Garnett ordered.

"BUT, Judge—" Netherdon sputtered.

"You're out of order, Mr. Netherdon. Control your client, Mr. Bagley," Judge Garnett instructed. And banged the gavel.

Two male deputies took Netherdon back into custody, and two female deputies ushered Shirley Millard from the courtroom.

For Blair, Landis, and Lauren, the arrest of Shirley Millard and the information obtained from West End Dodge on Wednesday had secured a successful conclusion to the investigation, so during Thursday's court recess they had scheduled and planned a party at the realty office to follow the close of the preliminary hearing on Friday.

The invitation list included the commonwealth attorney, the sheriff's staff, the emergency services staff, Della Dumond Shales and her husband Winston, Bob "Big Buck" Herman and his wife Betty, other Riverside Hunt Club members including Ross Peters and Denny Olsey, Toni Mathieson and several members of Roberta Dumond's church, Natty Lapplier and her family, Landis's friend Peter Mason, and Lauren's daughter Page.

Bartending behind the improvised bar, Landis and Peter Mason soon drew a small crowd.

"I hear you're a student at Sweet Briar College, Page. No boys there, so tell you what. I'll get you a job at Wintergreen during ski season, and next summer, too, for that matter. You can meet lots and lots of good-looking guys there! What say?"

"Cool!" Page returned enthusiastically.

"Speaking of 'guys', Page," Landis inserted, "what's going on with your mom and Denny Olsey?"

"She says they're just friends. But they're dating, and seems to me she's having a blast!" Page insinuated.

"I agree. And good for her! What kind of work does he do?" Blair asked, sidling in from the kitchen.

"Owns a trucking company," Landis answered.

"And just how did *you* learn that?" Blair quizzed.

"Ha! You should know. Her usual sleuthing, of course!" Peter laughed. "And speaking of that, call Ned Washburn over. I'd like to speak to him."

Landis took his request literally, shouting Washburn's name across the room. He approached, wearing an expression of trepidation.

"Don't be frightened, Ned, old buddy. It's no emergency. Just my friend here wants to talk to you," Landis explained.

Peter and Washburn mixed drinks for themselves and then maneuvered from behind the bar to have a chat. Minutes later Washburn raised his glass overhead, a motion to call the crowd's attention to his desire to propose a toast.

"To Lauren, actually to her nose, for the clue that nailed the case!" Washburn emoted, projecting to reach the ears of everyone in the room.

As "yea's" resounded, Lauren beamed and bowed. Standing close to her, Denny Olsey applauded heartily.

"What about me? I made the Richmond connection!" Landis pouted.

"Bless your heart, you surely did! Thanks. And thanks to Blair for finding and photographing tire marks at the Dumond home, thanks to Herman and fellow hunters for their successful search for Lauren, thanks to Natty Lapplier and her brother Eddie for finding Mrs. Dumond, thanks to the deputies and emergency service crews for their diligence and long hours, thanks to *everyone* who contributed to solving this case. We couldn't have done it without you all," Washburn declared.

"And thanks to you, Ned Washburn, for leading the effort," Richard Camfield saluted from across the room.

Momentarily startled, Washburn recovered quickly and tipped his glass in acknowledgement, but said nothing.

Blair smiled at both men, then summoned Lauren to assist her with replenishing hors d' oeuvre trays.

"Now, back to drinking and eating and being merry!" Peter Mason called loudly to re-direct everyone's attention, being sensitive to Blair's "situation" as Landis had relayed it to him—and responding to Landis's elbowing his ribcage.

"Belly up, boys!" Bob Herman whooped, signaling his hunting pals to rush the bar. "Let's everybody drink to the quick demise of 'Elmer Gantry' Netherdon!"

Washburn departed inconspicuously.

EPILOGUE

Monday morning Blair took her first cup of coffee, a cigarette, and her cell phone out to the patio garden. She dialed the sheriff's office and asked to speak to Washburn. A secretary routed her call to Sheriff Oakley.

"Uh, Mrs. Camfield, I'm sorry to report that Ned Washburn is no longer with us."

"No longer *with* you? I . . . I don't understand."

"Well, that makes two of us! It *was* kinda sudden. Late Friday he met with me and resigned, using his three weeks accumulated leave as notice time."

"Uh . . . huumm . . . Did he say why?"

"Something vague about needing a change. Said he was thinking of applying for a position with one of the northern Virginia law enforcement departments. Has family up that way, I believe. Can I help you with something?"

"Oh, no sir. No. It wasn't business."

"I see. Well, if we don't hear from him before then, he'll be back to testify at the Millard-Netherdon trial. You can contact him here at that time."

"Thank you. Good-bye." But even as she clicked off the phone, she knew that she would not try to contact Ned Washburn again.

Blair lighted her cigarette and walked out to her front pasture, lukewarm cup of coffee still in hand. Doby trotted beside her, sensing her mood and offering his presence to console her. She leaned on the board fence and gazed at the low-lying fog bank hanging over the pond. The scene reminded her of something she'd read in a British novel. The heroine in that story had viewed a similar scene while reflecting on a lost love.

"How bittersweet," she murmurred. And inhaled deeply.

The spell was soon broken. "Come on, Mom! Dad has your breakfast ready," Whitley yelled from the back porch.

Facing the bucolic scene a moment longer, Blair smiled wistfully. Then she patted Doby's head affectionately—and turned toward home.

BVG